No Greater Love

David Butler

Ward Wood Publishing

Published by Ward Wood Publishing
6 The Drive
Golders Green
London NW11 9SR
www.wardwoodpublishing.co.uk

The right of David Butler to be identified as the author of this work has been asserted by him in accordance with the Copyright, Designs and Patent Act, 1988. © David Butler 2013.

ISBN 978-1-908742-10-0

British Library Cataloguing in Publication Data. A CIP record for this book can be obtained from the British Library.

Designed and typeset in Garamond
by Ward Wood Publishing.

Cover design by Mike Fortune-Wood
from original artwork by © Thecult
Angel silhouette, black and yellow tonality, Paris
Supplied by agency: Dreamstime

Printed and bound in Great Britain by
Imprint Digital, Seychelles Farm,
Upton Pyne, Exeter EX5 5HY.

All the characters in this book are fictitious and any resemblance to actual persons (living or dead) or to institutions is purely coincidental.

No Greater Love

Out of the crooked timber of humanity, no straight thing was ever made.

Immanuel Kant

Contents

In the Name of God and of
the Dead Generations

No one remembered having seen the dead man get on the train. Most were too caught up in the electric rush to have glanced behind them. Others recalled fragments. Noticing how he'd jerked at every judder, the pair of tattooed lovers on a jaunt from Tallaght had assumed he was one more drunk. There was no shortage of drunks all over the seafront. The sombre Latvian couple who'd got on several rides later had supposed much the same, for all that he wasn't exactly slumped over. And the flock of prattling schoolgirls dressed up like Barbies breathlessly repeated how they'd thought the creepy guy in the hat was a part of the act! But no one could be found who'd actually seen the dead man climb on board. Even the old operator, a deadeye at spotting fare dodgers, simply could not say for how many turns the corpse had ridden the Ghost Train.

Drawn by the flicker of blue lights and rumour, pockets of onlookers began to idle in the precincts of the attraction. The night air grew charged with speculation. Giddy questions flittered about like bats. Twenty minutes on, why was the body still stuck there under a sheet in the end carriage? Why hadn't those two paramedics lifted it onto the stretcher? Weird, that. And what were the boys in blue up to, asking so many questions, scribbling away in their pads, looking all serious and jabbering into their walkie-talkies? Tell you one thing, there must've been something dead suspicious about the way he went, coz otherwise... You think so? Coz I'll tell you one thing, the way that siren shrieked inside there put the heart across me so it did. You ask me, he'd a weak heart. Would you ever cop on to yourself, and the place crawling with the guards! Hard to see how anyone could've sneaked up on him, but. Seeing how he was in the last carriage and everything. A priest, I heard he was, or a protestant. Doubt that! Come here, your one the ban-garda, now what exactly is she trying to find out from them schoolgirls and they what, twelve years of age? And what's the story with the blue and white tape all around the gaff like something out of CSI Miami?

By the time the detectives arrived, the rumours had taken on more definite contours. It seemed there was no sign at all of a wound. Nothing to say he'd been shot or stabbed, or strangled even. But he'd hardly died of heart failure either. The thing of it was, and this was seriously fecking weird if you thought about it, that body was already cold when they'd tried to rouse it. Your man there was saying. And for your information, the reason it's still up there propping up that white sheet like a pantomime ghost is on account of it's already stiff with rigor mortis. Now, that shook you! To move him out of that carriage now, you'd have to break both his legs so you would. So you're saying he must've been dead before ever they put him on the train? Must've been man! They must've killen him earlier on, an overdose of drugs maybe. Or poison. And then stuck him up there as a warning. How do you make that out? I'm only saying.

By the following morning, the bones of the prank were on every front page. The consensus was that medical students were behind it, up to no good as ever at this ragtime of the year. Why else would the corpse have been dressed in a shabby suit out of Oxfam, several sizes too large for it? Why did it sport a pair of golf shoes, but no socks; a Roman Catholic collar; and a battered panama pushed well down into its crown. The broadsheets had gone to print long before the state pathologist's preliminary findings were released, but already it was common knowledge that the cadaver had been deceased for a considerable period of time. Months, perhaps years. It had been washed, shaved entirely, and it smelled vaguely (though persistently) of formaldehyde. Not only that, but as one evening tabloid had it, that body apparently contained enough chemicals to have preserved an elephant, never mind a human!

There was only one problem with the supposition which laid the blame squarely at the foot of medical students. It was a problem that began to wax over the days to follow, even as the story faded to the sixth and seventh pages. There was no missing corpse. Not from Earlsfort Terrace; nor Trinity College; nor any of the University Hospitals; nor any Dublin undertaker's; nor the city morgue. The guards cast their net wider. Galway, Cork, Limerick, Waterford. Nothing. By the close of the second week, they'd cast it as far as the North. But it always came in empty. No morgue nor theatre on the island had registered the theft of a body.

In the absence of a cadaver, rumour began to take wing. A grave had been violated and the corpse dug up a bare day after it was buried. Someone's sister-in-law had seen the evidence with her own eyes out in Blessington cemetery. Not at all! The whole thing was a publicity gimmick on the part of the travelling fair; and the figure, a mummy that used to do the rounds with them in the days before law and custom began to frown on such fairground attractions. Nope. A reliable source told the brother the body had been smuggled in from Holland inside a refrigerated container so it had. Listen, word is, from someone who should know, it was trawled up in a dragnet down in Wexford years ago, and some loony-tunes taxidermist bought it on the q.t. and took the trouble to preserve it, only now he's after dying. Not a bit of it! Sure the body wasn't really a body at all. The whole thing was a hoax from start to finish, did you not know that?

The prank and the 1001 tales it gave rise to would likely have died a death if it hadn't been for the timely appearance of the second stiff. This discovery was made one Sunday morning by an elderly English couple out exercising their even more arthritic retriever on Killiney Hill. The bitch was of such a placid disposition that the couple were astonished, not to say mortified, when she began to bark furiously at the lady in the straw hat and feather boa who was sitting with her back to the Famine Folly, for all the world as if she were taking the April sun. But the dog wasn't fooled for a minute by the way the sea breeze animated the boa and set the pheasant feather atremble. The bitch's evidence was entirely olfactory.

A Deputy Commissioner put in an appearance on the six o'clock news that same evening, to appeal to whomever it was who was behind the sick joke to kindly desist and to have a consideration for matters of public hygiene, to say nothing of the trauma that might well ensue if a child or a person of delicate sensibilities were to stumble across a dead body in a public place. He further appealed to anyone who might have seen somebody acting suspiciously in the vicinity of the Famine Folly on Killiney Hill, or in the Bray area the previous month, or who might have any information as to the origin of the two bodies in question, to come forward, or indeed to contact the Garda Síochána on the confidential number that would be displayed on the screen at the end of the bulletin. Plenty came forward. The phone, as they say, scarcely stopped hopping. But as Monday dawned, the police were no nearer to solving the mystery.

Although the Deputy Commissioner had made no mention of it, it somehow became common knowledge that under the deceased's gloved hand there had lain a first edition hardback, unsigned, of Edna O'Brien's *A Pagan Place*. So much thought had gone into the lady's costume, and to the previous (a vicar, was it meant to be?), that the book could hardly be an accidental choice. By the time their appeal for information had graduated onto *Crimewatch* the following week, the Garda Síochána were sick, sore and tired of hearing theories relating to that particular detail. The appeal to the public was quietly relegated to the back burner.

The third corpse really put the wind up the public. Wild theories began to circulate once the facts came out. Having left their debs' dance up in Artane at blue o'clock in the morning, the four stragglers had been vexed when the final cab in the taxi rank made no move to take the place of its fellows once they'd been noisily engaged. After waving, whistling and dancing at it to no avail, the brashest of the debutantes, a girl well-known for taking no nonsense, took off the stilettos that were killing her so they were, marched barefoot as far as the driver's window and, when her impatient rat-a-tat with the heel of a shoe went entirely ignored, had yanked the door open, only to have the driver teeter rigidly out onto the tarmac. That the corpse appeared to be African in origin merely added to the sense of panic that gripped the city the following day.

For the first time, the rumours began to assume a supernatural hue. It was difficult to see how else the thing might have been pulled off. Unless someone had been crazy enough to manoeuvre the taxi into position while hunkered down in the passenger seat, with one hand reaching through the dead man's legs onto the accelerator, and the other on the steering wheel. But even so, how could they see to drive? Or when precisely did they slip away into the night? Was it before or after your man the Nigerian (was it?)

turned out to be a stiff? It made you think! Maybe there was something queer going on. First a parish priest, then your one reading a pagan book, and now this? A note on Twitter, uncorroborated but widely disseminated, maintained the taxi's licence no. was 666.

All that summer, the city was host to a plague of pranksters; teenagers and oddballs for the most part, who delighted in dressing up in morbid costumes, who prostrated themselves histrionically in doorways or draped themselves across public monuments. Their pictures propagated unchecked through Facebook and other social networks, and were widely imitated in cities not fortunate enough to have been visited by the dead. There were genuine false alarms, too. During the Bloomsday festivities, the body of a man washed up at the Forty Foot. The hands and feet had been bound. It was at first assumed to be the next term in the macabre series, until a Garda spokesman assured the public that the victim, a certain Matthew Kane, was well-known to the police. The drowning was the result of nothing more sinister than a gangland feud. Strange to say, the public were more disappointed than relieved. And all the while, the speculation grew more wild and feverish.

By the time the fourth and fifth corpses were found, sitting in casual embrace at the back of a cinema, there were broadcasts going out daily in seven European and two Asian languages. Dublin had quite simply never seen anything like it! The Minister for Tourism and Culture could only dream of such coverage during the long-planned-for 2016 celebrations. 'Publicity To Die For!' quipped one tabloid, not without sympathy. Then the dead lovers surfaced. The usherette of the Miramax, a pretty, foreign national with imperfect English and perfect teeth, said she'd 'grown suspicions not so much for they make no move leave once the light come up, but because for next five minute they make no move at all, and don't even take off 3D glasses.' A tub of popcorn on the girl's lap was two-thirds gone, the mobile in the boy's hand still turned to silent. Their tickets had been punched. Conspiracy theorists seized immediately on the film. It was a summer blockbuster about angels and demons battling for control of the New York Stock Exchange.

The sixth corpse may well have been the first. It was discovered fortuitously by an FBI agent named McMurrough who was visiting the old country for a second time, having tried unsuccessfully to trace his roots the previous year. No doubt it was his investigative instinct that made him look twice at the military figure lying on the stretcher in the waxworks museum off College Green. In any event, when he pulled the imitation Citizen Army cap from the head of the wounded Commandant, he revealed the same close-shorn scalp as had characterised the previous five cadavers (although the lady in Killiney had donned an elaborate wig). What made this discovery of particular interest was that, in anticipation of the centenary, the display had been put together some weeks prior to the funfair's arrival in Bray the previous March. Was it possible, then, that the corpse had faced down the dummy British firing squad in the full public glare for five months before anyone had noticed? On foot of that discovery, bizarre tales of shop-window mannequins that were no mannequins and night watchmen that were no watchmen began to do the rounds.

There was no seventh corpse. Perhaps there was never meant to be. One by one, the foreign journalists packed up their satellite vans and departed. As weeks gave way to months, and months to seasons, the memory of the giddiness the strange visitors had occasioned began to subside. Less and less were people inclined to share their theories, or to relate their own close encounters with the dead. The Garda forensics team assigned the thankless task of identifying the bodies was whittled down to two and, as the centenary year finally dawned, to a single junior member. The entire episode began to assume the contours of a national delusion, like Lord Lucan or the moving statues. At last, even BBC Northern Ireland lost interest. Weighing up the pros and cons as the floats motored past the GPO, the Minister for Tourism and Culture came to the view that, on balance, perhaps it was just as well. It wouldn't do at all to have the centenary celebrations disrupted by the untimely appearance of another bloody corpse.

Hen Night

The note must have been stuck to the underneath of her compact because it was precisely at the moment the reflected eye fixed her from out of its interior that the zigzag descent distracted her. It now sat perched at the edge of the washbasin, an innocuous butterfly. Eleanor looked back at the iris sustained in the circular mirror and watched the mascara stick approach. But before the heavy stamen had engaged the lashes she pulled the stick away and looked again at the piece of paper.

It was small, no bigger than a cigarette skin, and looked to have been torn from a larger page. Yet someone had taken the trouble to fold it. She wondered when it had become stuck to her compact. Could it have been in her handbag? But she shook her head, looked once more at the eye in the mirror, hesitated over touching the lower lash with the brush. Her own dark pupil appeared to be examining her. Abruptly, Eleanor snapped the compact shut and replaced it into her bag. The mascara stick followed. Now she had been piqued by curiosity.

She looked again at the folded paper that teetered at the edge of the washbasin. How could it have been in her handbag? That made no sense. She glanced once at the door of the bathroom, listened to the hum of conversation that still overpowered the music in the next room. Then she snatched it up. Her hand acted now as though the origami insect might at any minute take flight. She opened it, smoothed out the folds, and allowed her eye run over the four short words scribbled along its interior. Too late, as though it had just stung her palm, she flung the note from her.

In the bathroom mirror a paralysed figure leaned towards her. A comic figure in bridal veil and Learner's plate. Her mouth was open, a perfect O. Her eyes, wide-open. But Eleanor was not looking at this woman. Eleanor was staring at where the note had fallen into the wash-hand basin. It lay sustained on the soapy skin of water, face down, the words a line of dissolving shadow showing through wet paper. Four syllables, thirteen letters. Their force had struck her solar plexus so unexpectedly that she could not breathe.

It was a full minute before she regained enough composure to consider what she had read. Of course it was a joke, a sick joke, but which of her girlfriends could have been so malicious? Who would have acted in such bad taste? One corner of the paper had already dipped beneath the water's surface, the ink slowly dissolving into its warm undertow. Carefully, forensically, Eleanor lifted it out and laid it onto a white hand-towel. The ink had faded and spread like a lichen, but the trace remained legible. She looked again at the sentence, the thirteen letters, executed in a hand that was studiously casual.

I slept with Dan.

'We were beginning to think you were never coming out!' This was Chantal, Michelle's younger sister. Scarcely twenty, she was already tipsy. But Michelle, looking up at her from the sofa, addressed her with concern.

'Are you all right, El? You're very pale.'
The conversation in the room was sporadic now that the music had finished, and Eleanor felt that all eyes were watching her. She managed to raise a smile for their benefit.

'No, I'm fine. Really.'
'She's got cold feet!' Miriam – voluble, laughing Miriam. 'She's scared stiff so she is!' And the whole room was suddenly laughing. The bottles of wine were laughing, the cds were laughing, the tortilla dips and the photographs and the potted plants were laughing, the poster by Matisse of the lovely odalisque, it too was laughing.

One of the girls attended to the music system and the speakers cackled back into life. Another, Katie, with red devil's horns and a tail, began to dance close and sexy with Michelle's huge teddy bear.

'Come on! You need to get one of these inside you.' A winking eye. 'Dutch courage!'

So that she took the glass that was being pressed into her hand and, touching the brim to her lip, she allowed the volatile spirit to fill her lungs. Was it brandy? Eleanor glanced timidly around the faces that were admiring her, the eyes that were encouraging her. One pair among them must know of the somersault that had sacked her world. But then Michelle manoeuvred her out with one hand on the shoulder and another close about the waist, and

16

before they left the flat they began a dance that was even more provocative than Katie's.

How was it that she had got through the meal? The table, long and narrow, about which banter flew and jokes and ribald comments; the long table, with its closeness and deception and devious scrutiny. Four of the girls now had red devils' horns and Michelle, the white ears of a rabbit. A Playboy bunny. Her own veil was a blur in the periphery of her vision.

I slept with Dan.

And she had no memory of having ordered or even having looked at the menu, so that when there was a mix-up, first over the starters and then again over the main courses, Miriam had laughed out 'Poor thing! She's so much in love, she's off her food so she is!', 'love' and 'food' beaten flat by her Ulster accent. And Michelle, who was returning after a cigarette, had added from behind her: 'For once Miriam has a point. I've never seen you make such a poor effort at a marinara.' And then Katie had shouted 'Oh my God El you never told us you were pregnant!' and the shrieks that followed disturbed the other tables so that the waiters frowned at their party.

Juvenile Chantal, giggling Chantal, was sitting diagonally opposite, and the Chianti had quite obviously gone to her head because as the deserts were arriving her flighty hand upset a wineglass. A huge stain spread over the cloth like a shadow, and a trickle dribbled onto Eleanor's thigh before she had a chance to move out of its path. 'Oh my God I'm so sorry!' But Michelle, calm as a nurse, was able to apply a salt compress which lifted the worst of the crimson out of the silk.

Which of the eyes was watching with low malice?

It was late and the dance-floor was far too crowded. A couple of foreign boys were busy entertaining two of the she-devils, but the rest of her group was ranged about a stand to the left of the bar. Drinks in various shapes and colours overpowered the miniature surface. But her girlfriends were tired of being jostled, and the mood was subdued.

I slept with Dan. Each time it returned with the force of a blow.

Then at some point Michelle had taken her by the arm and steered her across the dance-floor in the direction of the restrooms. *What in God's name do you pair get up to in there together? The sorority of the toilet!* That was Dan all over, the crow's feet and the squinting eyes. He was forever goading Michelle. He got on so well with all of her girlfriends. Only her brother had never warmed to his easy manner. So was it possible … no! No! Eleanor could not let her imagination go there. She shut her eyes and drove down the sudden rebellion in her entrails. Not Dan.

And after they had queued, the dank, buttocky closeness of the bathroom, so heavy with sprays, made her feel faint. The truth is she was not used to drink. Like a true friend Michelle had seen that the others had not pressed too many spirits on her, but there was only so much that one could do. This was meant to be Eleanor's night.

'Talk to me, El. What is it? You haven't been yourself all evening.'

Michelle was standing at the wash-basin beside her. As she waited for Eleanor to reply she began to touch up her lips, kissing a tissue paper and then pouting provocatively at her reflection. She was very attractive, Michelle, when she made the effort.

'I don't know. I…'

And suddenly she was sobbing. Great gobs of anxiety swelled up from her guts and poured out of her mouth. She teetered, gripped the wash-basin. She felt her friend's arms steady her. 'For God's sake what is it? Ellie!' But throat and lungs were racked with spasms and she could not speak. She opened her mouth, and no air came from her lungs. No word could pass through the stricture in her throat. It was as if terror had seized her.

Outside. It is almost three o'clock.

'Can you talk?'

'…'

'I'm sorry, you're breaking up on me.'

'…'

'No. Listen. Will you ring me back?'

There is too much bustle and noise on the streets, and the connection is fragile. Brittle. The girl in the white rabbit ears glances quickly at the anonymous faces that grin past. Then she looks instead to the squat phone that nests in her palm. Even outside, even at this late hour, she is reluctant to raise her voice.

18

Perhaps the walls will overhear.

She lights a cigarette and glances back towards the bouncer. As she exhales blue smoke into the night air she thinks over the evening's vicissitudes. She thinks of the moment that her best friend disappeared into her bathroom before they left the flat. All the while Eleanor was in there, a rage of butterflies had troubled her stomach.

She draws again on the cigarette and squints in the direction of the club. She does not want to think about what she has done. She does not want to think. Her eyes deflect to the phone. What words will she say to him? How will she have the nerve to tell him?

She is becoming tense. She flicks away the cigarette, half-smoked. Inside her, the rage of butterflies is relentless. She glances hurriedly at the entrance to the club. But if Eleanor were to step out, now, this minute? Could she admit? Beg her forgiveness? Go back?

A vibration shocks her hand. A light tenses, dilates, bickers.

She raises the phone and reads, in panic, in relief, his flashing name.

No Greater Love

They say that I am an evil woman. An ogre. They say that, ten years ago, I was seized by a jealous rage so powerful that I strangled to death my only daughter. Why shouldn't they say it? After all, I have never denied the charges that were levelled against me, and neither did I appeal when I was sentenced to life imprisonment. And how they've rejoiced, the jackals of the tabloids, to see how ten years of prison life have robbed me of my beauty and left me an old, old woman. You wouldn't think it, but next year is my *fortieth* birthday, though it's true you might mistake me now for a woman of sixty. Nadya would have been twenty-three today, if she was alive. If no *crime* had been committed … but enough of that! Of that they know nothing.

No, it's not the prison life, as they would have it, that has stolen my youth and greyed my hair. It is not the heavy grind of routine, nor the scorn of the world, nor the faceless, changeless future that has made me so old before my time. No, that honour … (for surely such an honour must be acknowledged, must have its author) … that honour, I say, must go solely to Mikhail Mikhailovitch, whose living hatred has been the bane and the comfort of my life here. His hatred poisons my dreams and defeats my spirit as surely as it has nourished and vindicated me. But you will see. You will see.

It was a wild November evening when I was first presented to Mikhail Mikhailovitch Sirhin. '*M. M. Sirhin, pianist*'. How modest the card read! Of course he wasn't famous then, or at least he was unheard of outside the closed circle of the Leningrad Academy, and his defection to the West had been such a low key affair that the national papers had scarcely remarked on it. The first thing that struck me about him on the day we were introduced was his inordinate reserve, his cold haughtiness. This seemed so out of keeping with his cheap, battered shoes and his childish English that I could not restrain myself, and burst out laughing even as I shook hands with him. I was scarcely more than a child myself, and the new piano tutor cut quite a comic figure in our somewhat formal household.

But there was very little that was comic in the life of Mikhail Mikhailovitch. He was a tall man, not unattractive, and there was a remarkable self-assurance in his hard blue eyes. His trousers were scarcely long enough to conceal mismatched socks, and his raincoat had a tear that ran along the collar. Yet he seemed to treat my parents with disdain, and glowered at me whenever I smiled at the frequent mistakes in his English. The fact is, he saw his poverty as an irrelevance, nothing more than a ragged cover drawn over his immense talent, and he grew indignant when others failed to see this. My parents undoubtedly could see it, but I was fourteen years old and to me he was an absurd and amusing newcomer, one whose speech was as ragged as his dress. Each time he fixed his eyes on me, however, I felt my ears burn.

He had at this time been in England for seven months – all this I learned much later – having fled Russia shortly after his wife's suicide. To this day I know little about her, except that she was originally from Prague, and that she swallowed an entire bottle of bleach when life with her Russian husband in distant Leningrad became too much for her. I never managed to learn her name, although I occasionally saw her photograph in his wallet. She was dark-eyed, petite, ten years younger than he. I have always imagined, from her dark, sad eyes, that she must have loved him with the same desperation, or desperate isolation, with which he infected me. I know now that it was my own soul that stared silently from the pitch black eyes in his wallet photograph.

I was fourteen, but I was no fool. My mother had forecast I would be a beauty, and though I was young and without experience, I sensed already the fascination that I induced in men. My own cousin, twenty years old and on leave from the army, had stuttered and blushed when he'd tried to talk to me the summer before. Yet how quickly did this clumsy, arrogant man, more than twice my age, gain a hold on my thoughts and a grip on my heart which has never since eased off. From the first he was a tyrant, staring coldly from indecipherable, northern eyes and demanding an impossible perfection. And how *his* self-belief dwarfed my own, searing it until I could no longer bear the sight of a music score, much less give life to one on a grand piano. Finally he broke me, but by that time I was already his lover, and five months pregnant.

21

His monstrous self-sufficiency became even more entrenched as the years passed and recognition was afforded him by the world (make no mistake, his talent is remarkable and even now has only been partly revealed or understood). But it would have been so much easier for me if he mistreated me; I could have put up with that joyfully, if only he would have let me *matter* to him. If only he would have acknowledged that I ever *existed* for him. Perhaps he loved me in his own way, if Mikhail Mikhailovitch were ever able to feel love, but he certainly never *needed* me, this man whose life was all that I lived for.

But I am being unfair. He always loved Nadya. From the first day I'd told him that I was pregnant with his child, I slowly faded and ceased to exist for him, but here was *life*, here was the thing itself. He took an interest in her from that moment right up to the day that they found her strangled in our home, and had watched her with that same intense, searing gaze that he had once, so long ago, turned on me. It was the gaze with which he had long ago forged the hard perfection of his own talent, and which would in turn bring Nadya Mikhailovna to perfection. And for Mikhail Mikhailovitch, that gaze was love itself.

With me he had been a slave-driver, a monster, but with our daughter his tyranny took on a different form. He could extend or withhold affection with the same facility that he could play upon a keyboard, fondling her or being cold to her without uttering so much as a single syllable of reproach. I watched his love blossom suddenly into laughter as she gained each grade and moved from success to success, and the dark despair that would fall between them when she failed to live up to his expectations of her. I stood on the sidelines. I watched. I waited.

The era of *glasnost* arrived, and Mikhail Mikhailovitch Sirhin was invited to return to the Leningrad Academy for a performance that would mark the culmination of his career to date. The Minister for Culture himself would be there, with who knows how many other notables of the Soviet World. And yet, with a defiant quirkiness that had come increasingly to characterise his performances, *Mikhail Mikhailovitch refused to go*. The reason? His daughter, the precocious cellist Nadya Mikhailovna Sirhin, who was to perform on that same night for the title of 'Young

Musician of the Year', would perform faultlessly only under his loving gaze. The notables of Soviet Russia could simply wait.

For thirteen years I had watched. For thirteen years I had waited silently as his monstrous love tried to mould our daughter in his image. And she had always striven to earn that love. She had driven herself, she had practised ceaselessly, and she had wilted when she had fallen short of that which the pale fire of his eyes demanded. She was thirteen years old, a year younger than I was when Mikhail Mikhailovitch's cold eyes had begun to burn me. I tried to offer our child love on her own terms, when she cried at night or when she stared vacantly from the living-room window, but I scarcely existed any more for her than I did for her father.

Now at least he hates me, though that misdirected hatred is often more than I can bear. Yet what would he be today, if I'd simply left her?

You see, the truth of the matter is very different to that which they wrote in their papers. I am no 'evil woman'. The truth is a precious item that I have twisted and concealed, buried with the body of our daughter so that Mikhail Mikhailovitch will never ruin himself on it. On the evening of the fourteenth, a wild November evening, I found the body of Nadya Mikhailovna hanging from the living-room chandelier, still warm, and with a note clenched in her right fist. The note bore the single Russian word '*nyeudachnitsa*', which is to say failure, so that there can be no doubt to whom it had been addressed. She'd even used one of his belts as a noose. What amazes me even now is that throughout the next half hour I remained calm, more perfectly calm than I had been for many years. I suppose it's because all that I did was animated by a single, all-powerful conviction. *Mikhail Mikhailovitch must never know.*

Perhaps I don't need to tell the rest. They say that the greatest love a man can have is to die for someone else. But how much harder, how much purer is it to live on in someone's hatred just so that they will never know the crime that they themselves are guilty of? Could he have lived, having burned the only person he had ever really loved? Could I have lived, seeing him finally destroyed by the terrible image of his perfection? What else had I to live for?

I cut the body down – luckily, her neck wasn't broken, but rather she had been strangled by the belt that she had used – and when I had removed every trace from the living-room, I dragged my daughter upstairs into her bedroom, bound her hands, and wrapped the belt she'd choked upon several times about the bedstead. I brought a paperweight down heavily upon her temple, to intimate a struggle, and tore the sleeve of her blouse. The note I tore up and ate.

Mikhail Mikhailovitch Sirhin postponed the Leningrad performance for eighteen months, all told, but has played twice a year there ever since, to great critical acclaim.

Unless He is Born Again

Hoisted onto the wall he hesitates. Night has turned the river to marble. Will the plunge even break the puckered surface? *Mustn't. Mustn't think.* Eyes shut, hands fast in pockets, he levers himself into free-fall. Then...

...tumbled head over heels by the current the body struggles. Arms thrust sideways into the opaque turmoil. Legs pedal out and down, to where instinct cries is down. Eyeball can no more penetrate the murk than eardrum the muted, turbulent din. *Mustn't. Mustn't.* Momentarily, he quells the body's mutiny. He holds still. He feels his limbs drift through the freezing and violent waters. Coldness grips vicelike, and vicelike tightens. It clutches until mouth screams to discharge its burden of air. *Mustn't.* When knee and elbow buffet along the bottom silt, he allows the mouth to open. He holds the meniscus as long as lung can bear it. Then he screams a great bubble into the icy murk. He is imagining the plate he saw in Mahood's book: a soul escaping its corpse.

But the instant the first glut of clayey water hits his epiglottis, great spasms seize his body. Now the struggle is with terror. In blind terror, hands tug at the coat that is drowning them. In terror, legs kick out. In terror head rolls and butts until for one brief instant his face breaks the surface and mouth can bite off a dark gobbet of air. Throat gags, splutters, but gullet holds down the wet air against its coughing. The river, a vast beast, drags him under once again. Now his struggle is with the river. Suddenly united, body and soul find their orientation in the submarine dark: which way is up; which down. The gobbet of oxygen is too fast exhausted, but as he plunges it a third time into his rebellious lungs his hands cease tugging at the coat. His fingers grow instantly subtle. They tunnel down into the pockets, to where the flatirons are weighing downwards. These irons they delve out and, releasing them, he kicks out at the soft mud already buffeting beneath his legs.

Slowly, painfully, he rises through the waters.

This is not the first time his body has betrayed him. Not by a long shot.

25

April. A figure is loitering in the vicinity of the bus station of a provincial town. He's not the only stranger in the bus yard. There are strangers with almost every arrival and departure. There's nothing about this man to suggest he's a foreigner. But all the same, something in his aspect attracts suspicious looks. Perhaps it's the slightly dishevelled coat, missing the third button. Perhaps the eyes, raw with insomnia. Perhaps the disreputable bag in which he totes…what? Clothes? A few books? The residue of a life.

Opposite the bus yard is a sign: *JJ Mullin, Building Contractor.* He will call himself JJ.

There's a suggestion of rain. But although the yard is open to the elements, JJ is in no hurry to move on. An hour passes. The woman with the horn-rimmed spectacles behind the sweets and newspaper counter has been aware of this man for the longest time. She singles him out with a nod to anyone who dawdles about her stand. Who is he? Why doesn't he move on? He doesn't look like he's waiting for anyone, much less a connecting bus. What can he want here?

Him. That man.

JJ is aware of her, and of her less than kind attentions. He does nothing either to attract them or to assuage them. But he's in no hurry to move on. It's JJ's fourth provincial town in as many years.

'Go on Father. Ask him what he wants.'

Mahood smiles to himself. *Father.* Sure he's never been a priest! But the rumour has persisted in the town since first he retired here. There are those like Bridget Dowling who cling to it like a superstition.

He follows her scowl towards the man on the bench. Mahood has nothing to fear from a down-and-out. In his middle years, he worked the toughest doss houses of inner city Dublin, did she not know that? Drunks! Hopeless cases! By God, he can remember the smell as if it was yesterday. Poverty has a smell, Bridget. The scleroses. The musty clothes. The ruined bladders.

He'll be living here seven years this September, and still they call him Father. He that was far from being a priest! But Mahood knows, too, that the Lord protects his own. And if he thought about it deeply enough, it's the Lord's work he's about. 'All right,' he smiles, grimly. 'All right, Bridget. Leave it to me.'

The woman in the horn-rimmed spectacles returns his smile to his face. But it puckers up like a prune the minute he's turned his back to her. What if the scene was to turn ugly? What if that other … *so-and-so* was to turn nasty? And to a priest! Would she have done better not to say it to him? Would she have done better to wait until one of the bus drivers was knocking around the place? Because you never can tell…

JJ watches the old, desiccated man in the black coat approach him. He is tall. He is gaunt. His eyes are pale and severe. JJ moves his centre of gravity forwards on the bench. His hand moves to the bag.

Because you never can tell…

JJ has met charitable men before. Women, too, though he's always found women wary of him. As though they got a scent off him that put them ill at ease. Or else the opposite, and then of course they're too nosy. There's nothing in between, with women. But he's never met a man like Mahood before. Within two days Mahood has arranged digs for him with a Mrs Flynn, and what's more, covered the cost of it. Within a week, a position behind the till in a charity shop. Normally there would be no question of a salary. But on top of the board and lodging, Mahood allows him forty euro a week. Forty euro, until such time as he has sorted out his dole money.

Mahood had winked when he heard the accent. 'You're a Dub then?' But beyond that he has asked him nothing, not even his full name. Or his real name. Has he realised how impossible it will be for JJ to sign on the dole? Maybe. A nuance in his pale eyes suggested it.

No, he's never met a character like Mahood before. Who knows? He might even get to trust the man.

It's Mahood who makes the first move.

One day, a propos of nothing, while they're alone and sorting through a late delivery of clothes and books and odds and ends, the old man begins to talk freely.

27

'I suppose you've heard them call me Father?'

JJ shrugs.

'Father!' he laughs. 'Of course I was never married, that must be what's behind it!'

JJ merely grunts, busy with the task to hand. He is moving a number of flatirons into the storeroom. What are they used for?

'When I was young,' Mahood goes on when JJ returns, his pale eyes candid, 'd'you know, I took a most violent dislike to the clergy. And in all these years I've never warmed to them. I was a CBS boy.'

He stops until the other looks at him, then shakes his head. It's as much as to say, and we both know what that means!

'One of their famous Industrial Schools. A place whose name to be honest with you I don't care to remember. I was convinced it was a purgatory on earth, and every Christian Brother, a devil sent to torment us. Ach, I'm sure it was probably no worse than anywhere else. By all accounts, there was all sorts of violence and carry-on in those days.'

He pauses. He's leafing through one of the hardbacks he has pulled from a sack, a book of religious iconography. One image shows the soul escaping, like a speech bubble, the mouth of a dying man. He turns it towards JJ and … does he wink? Or is it a trick of the light? Either way, he tosses the volume nonchalantly onto the growing heap of books.

'But there was one character there who particularly got my goat. A Br Coyle. Carrots, we used to call him, on account of the hair, though to tell you nothing but the God's truth, it was already more grey than orange in my day. And I've yet to see a grey carrot! Now this Br Coyle was what you'd call one walking bastard. For years I've thought about this, and there's no other word for his carry-on. I don't say he was…*that way*. But the man was a born sadist, and one walking bastard!'

JJ scarcely looks at the other. But there's something in his movements that indicates the intensity with which he's listening.

'Now, the mistake this Br Coyle made is, one fine day, and this when I was a lad of no more than fourteen mind, he took the leather strap to me for something that I never done. A fellow called Roche, a right little Cabra gurrier, had tried to set fire to a pile of wood shavings behind the lathe and Carrots, on account of

I'd been caught smoking the previous week and on account of he had it in for me anyways, took it into his head to give me an unmerciful beating. And this before the entire woodwork class. I was an inch or two taller than him, but with what they fed you on, I was like a pull-through for a rifle. And besides, everyone was so scared stiff of Carrots that there'd never once been a case of anyone standing up to him, least ways not in all the years I was there.'

There is a pause. JJ realises he has stopped moving. At once he throws himself into the task in hand with renewed vigour. There are only a couple of irons remaining to be moved.

'So that was all very well. It wasn't me, Brother, says I. Sure I might as well have been talking to that pile of books there! He pulls at one of my hands, and draws back the leather over the shoulder with his beady eyes glittering like the cat that's caught hold of a mouse. Oh by Christ something broke in me at that moment. I couldn't tell you what it was, JJ, but something snapped. First I stopped his hand with the leather and then, when I saw his face grow white with the anger, before ever he had a chance to bawl into my face, a hand of mine had found an old chisel that was lying on the worktop beside us, and I drove it with all the force I could muster right there into his thigh. Right there, do you see?'

Now JJ looks at him. It's not what he was expecting to hear. Not from this priestly man.

'Now to cut a long story short, the next thing of course, it got infected! Blood poisoning, if you don't mind! It still wasn't right by the time yours truly was standing before the magistrate for sentencing. So the long and the short of it is, I spent the balance of my teenage years up above inside Patrick's on the North Circular Road.'

There's a silence. Is he waiting for JJ to ask him something? But how can JJ think anything beyond an infected wound, there on the thigh?

'To tell you nothing but the God's own truth, it was the makings of me. I came out of juvie with two things. A lifelong hatred of the clergy, and a mission in life to prove to them bastards that I was worth every bit as much as they were.'

JJ looks at him, this desiccated figure in greys and blacks. For the first time, he allows himself to smile. 'And they call *you* Father!'

'And they call *me* Father.'

But the eyes are too candid. JJ looks away. 'And so?'

'At nineteen I was out on the street, and more on my own than I'd ever been. If you think it was hard in those times getting a start when you've no relations, try it when you've a criminal record! So I signed up, I joined the army. I mean of course the British Army, sure ours is only boy scouts. It was the only place that would have me! I'd no more interest in guns nor fighting than that broom over there. But I'll say this for them, it was the nearest thing to a family I ever had. It was a place you belonged, d'you know what I'm saying to you? And it was the same British Army that give me the chance to do what I done up in the tenements of Dublin, once I'd served out my years with them. The early pension, you see.'

JJ looks at him for a long time without speaking. Their work is finished. They make sure all the electrics are off, then move to the door. It is JJ who's been entrusted by this stranger with the keys. As they make to go their separate ways, JJ declares, 'I was a maths teacher, would you believe that now?' Then he snorts, and walks into the night.

This is how they go on.

Mahood never asks more than JJ is willing to impart. He never asks why he left the teaching. He never asks what caused the two scars, scored by a Stanley knife, to the left side of his throat. He never asks why a smell like sweetened grass often disguises the whiskey on his breath. Still, by degrees, he finds out that JJ was married. That he is separated. That there's a child, unlikely to be his. He hasn't seen her since she was a toddler.

What he doesn't find out, though it might be guessed, is that it's in the mess of a disintegrating marriage that things began to go radically wrong for JJ. He doesn't find out how her first infidelity led, indirectly, inexorably, to the night when the façade of his world finally caved in.

He doesn't find out about the disgrace.

One would have to go back five years for that. One would have to go back to a windscreen drenched with blue, flickering lights. One would have to go back to the gloved hand tapping on the window, and the alcohol heavy on his breath. The maths teacher's breath. One would have to go back to the schoolgirl drunk in the passenger seat beside him, sixteen years of age. And then to a man, sitting alone on Dun Laoghaire pier in the drowning rain. He no longer has a driver's licence. He no longer has a job. He no longer has a marriage.

JJ has been in the town for five months before he all but succumbs. It is not the first attack. Not the first temptation. But by now, he's begun to feel secure enough in his routines here that loneliness has stirred and begun to gnaw.

There's nothing so voracious as loneliness. Nothing so tyrannical. More than once, it has driven him to the edge of madness.

His pace slows as he nears the cries in the park. It's a pleasant area, raised some yards above a bend in the river. The convent girls cross over the footbridge, here. At three, the mothers chat on benches and release their children into the play area. Their screams of delight and alarm fill the air like the screams of the swallows scything the river. He is at the other side of the wall. He is filled with giddiness. He is filled with self-loathing.

He looks about him, a drowning man. How can anyone understand what's driving the pounding of his heart? Or understand what flightiness is coursing frantically through his veins? How, if they haven't teetered on the brink? It's a form of vertigo. It's the giddy urge to feel oneself trip over the edge. He senses the intoxicating moment of weakness, just a half second before the downward plunge. All restraint, so painstakingly built up, all willpower, all self-respect is just on the point of collapse. Then it will happen. JJ knows he will realise, with a gorgeous panic, that the moment is already passed when all could have been saved.

But not today!

He is running. His head tilts forwards and he races along the street as if the cries of the children are demons pursuing him. He runs until he has made the door of Mrs Flynn's and only then, though before opening it, only then does he dare to look behind him. The street is empty.

Once he is safe in his room he pulls his case from beneath the bed and starts to throw his possessions from the wardrobe into a frantic pile beside it. But it's no good. He needs to expend energy. He's desperate to punish his body. He longs for the nerve to hurl himself headfirst against the walls. Instead, he sits on the edge of the bed and stares at the pile of clothes and books, unseeing, hearing nothing but the hammering of his heart.

Loneliness can drive a man to despair. It sits on brood over his emptiness, and who knows what might hatch. Loneliness can drive a man to extremes: to self-abuse; to suicide; or violence; or even, most awful of all, to degradation.

But today, it will drive him in a different direction.

'You see these?' he says, his fingers touching the twin scars at the base of his neck. 'That was the first time. Ha ha! Sure I'd no idea what I was doing man. On that occasion, it was a failure of the will, pure and simple. I poked, and I prodded, and I shut my eyes. But the hand just wouldn't pull the damn thing beyond where you can see. It wasn't even the pain of it! It was, how can I explain it to you?'

Mahood's eyes are by far the most youthful of his features. They mock the wrinkles that surround them. 'I think you put it very well. A failure of the will. Sure I saw it any number of times in the army.'

'All I know is, when I knew I couldn't go through with it, I hurled the knife into the sea as if it had just bit me. Tell me honestly, would you not call that cowardice?'

Mahood considers this. The strange individual standing before him has given him no earthly reason for his flirtations with suicide, nothing beyond the bald refrain: 'I'm a fucking monster!' He calls to mind the face of a Derry recruit, McCrery?, McKinley?, who blew his brains out in Malaysia when homesickness and bullying got too much for him. 'I wouldn't call it cowardice. Have you considered, JJ, maybe the cowardly thing would have been to have gone through with it?'

JJ looks away. This sounds to his ears a platitude, pure and simple. A plaster, to cover up the septic wound. A minute goes by, two. But he doesn't want to let this chance escape.

'The second time, I tried it with pills. I knew well I'd never have the nerve to do myself harm directly. I mean slashing the wrists, or throwing the body from a roof. But this time it was my stomach let me down. Call it a failure of the guts, ha ha! I woke up in a pool of vomit, and a headache that lasted for three days. For three days man!' He looks up at the other and screws his eyes. 'Do you know what it is? I think, no matter what the mind might decide, I think the body clings to life like it was a wild animal.' This thought is met with silence. 'Three days I had that headache.'

'And when was that?'

'When? Oh, a year ago now. Fifteen months.'

'And you've been ok since then?'

He lies awake, staring at the ceiling. His eyes are filling once more with the grit of insomnia. He's like a gambler who has played his last card, the card he had held back all this time for fear of playing it. Of course, it was no sooner played than lost. 'And you've been ok since then!' If he'd been able to ask that, Mahood hadn't understood a single word!

I can't go on like this, he mutters for the thousandth time. It's a statement that, over the months, over the years, has lost every contour of meaning.

But at what stage was the game lost? At what stage did the progression, the descent, become inevitable? Where was the lost trick that cost the game? Other people seem to get on with life. But he's replayed the sequence so often in his head that it's a track worn smooth. There are no longer any features for his imagination to grip onto, no alternatives to be played out. In the early days, he would imagine all sorts of scenarios. They crowded his head; every 'what-if' a nail driven into the past so vividly, so mercilessly, that in the end they paralysed him. But now (now!) he can scarcely tell anymore what had actually been said, and what done. If he tries to conjure the past, it's only because the future frightens him. It is barren, bereft of possibilities.

He shuts his eyes and makes a vow out loud. Tomorrow night I'll take those blasted irons from the storeroom. I'll make an end of it!

The headlights of a passing car glide over the head and muddied shoulders struggling through a great bank of reeds. Instinctively, it freezes. Instinctively, though the man has no strong desire to hide, the body shrinks down in the reeds until tyres have hissed past and the red lights have diminished around the corner in the direction of the distant town. The driver has noticed nothing, and the hum of the engine recedes into the darkness.

It is quiet. Not so much as a dog bark. Only the sibilance of the river, and the wind in the trees.

His body struggles rapidly through the reeds. Once they found he was in his depth, the legs hastened him forwards, and now hands clutch at everything that grows from the banks. It's a mad scramble to get out of the river.

He levers his body, the coat heavy with water, onto the bank.

He lies on his back and faces the stars. A shiver runs through him. He is cold, but it's delicious to be alive. He can feel his heart thumping so hard that through the coat it must be visible. He turns his head and retches a gob of river water into the grass. He wipes his mouth and stares again at the constellations. Thin screeds of cloud blowing across the sky give them the appearance that they are moving. And he knows by their apparent motion that he is alive. The clay, damp and uneven beneath him, presses the message into his back. Even the wind, which has such an edge it could skin him, tells him he is alive.

After five minutes, when the cold begins to rack him and the shudders become painful, he sits up. He looks about. Then slowly, achingly, he gets to his feet.

'All right,' he says, 'all right.'

And he sets off towards the lights of the distant town.

How Blaithin Met Zbigniew

The bracelet was already inside Blaithin's bag when she noticed the security guard's eyes in the mirror. Had he just shaken his head at her? Her heart, which had already been flitting like a bird inside a cage, pulsated.

What to do? What to do?

Her eyes raced around the department store. The assistant was still busy with the African woman. Twenty yards beyond stood the main exit. But the guard was at the same distance from that escape. Without the slightest doubt, he'd intercept her. She recalled a side entrance. But that was somewhere beyond Lingerie. By the time she'd swept past the rails and mannequins, the man would be on top of her.

What to do?

In a heartbeat her eye jumped to the changing rooms by the lift. She had the head start needed to take refuge there. Once inside, she'd simply lose the damned chain! But her stomach plummeted. Both the tiny rooms were occupied. Worse, there was a queue: a rotund lady with a stern face; a pregnant teenager with pushchair and iPhone.

What to do?

Blaithin's heart battered at her throat as though it, too, wanted to escape. Her breath came in gasps. For a protracted moment, she again met the guard's eyes in the mirror. Then, unbearably, she saw him detach himself from the wall. He was manoeuvring between her and the main exit. She'd have to act now! *Now!*

Head down, she bundled herself in the vague direction of Lingerie. One hand slipped into her bag, an ethnic affair her flatmate Sonja had brought back from Peru. But Blaithin's fingers must have grown stupid. They couldn't find the thing! In a panic, they burrowed past the compact and the Silk Cut and under the fat purse and through the headscarf. There was no bracelet anywhere!

A memory wouldn't let go. During the Christmas Sales, a store detective had caught her red-handed. She'd tapped her shoulder a bare second after Blaithin stepped out onto the street, and she'd frogmarched her upstairs to the Floor Manager. Blaithin had been lucky. There would be no prosecution. But that was only after her mother had been telephoned. For your *motherr's* sake, the manageress nasally intoned, *this toime* the *univahrrsity* need *not* be *infohrrmed.*

True, it was a different department store. But Blaithin couldn't go through that ordeal again. *What to do?* She was scared stiff to look behind her, terrified to gauge the bare seconds that remained her. Frantically, she turned the bag upside-down. She tugged at its innards. She shook it. Something hit her foot and rolled away; not the bracelet. It must be tangled in the lining.

'Miss!' a man's voice spoke, behind her.

At that precise moment, the lift opened. With a coolness that afterwards astonished her, she waited for the doors to be on the point of closing before she skipped inside. She fisted the buttons as the doors juddered, half-closed, hesitated, jerked, and at last came together. After an unbearable delay, the floor moved.

Blaithin had no time to be relieved. She held the bag upside-down at eye-level. The purse fell out and slapped off her leg. In a single movement, without looking, she'd retrieved it. The scarf was dangling like a silken entrail. She rummaged past it and pushed at the floor of the bag. The bracelet was nowhere to be found, and the lift was slowing. Eyes wide, she pulled out the headscarf. She shook it. The doors were already shuddering. Nothing! In desperation she turned the scarf about. And there it was! Thin, glinting, snagged on some loose threads. She tugged, twice, and felt the threads or the catch snap. The doors were wide open by the time the chain slid from her hand.

As Blaithin hurried from the lift, she could sense the security guard. Eyes fixed on the far wall, she pushed on. 'Miss!' he said, quietly. She halted. 'Miss, I think you dropped this.' The floor of her stomach cavorted. She could scarcely breathe. Fighting down a sob of frustration, she turned to face him. His blue gaze was cool, his face supercilious. 'No,' she gasped. 'I didn't.'

He ignored her protest. Without his taking his eyes from her eyes, she felt his hand take hers. She felt an object pressed into it, and her fingers being folded over that object. She shut her hot eyes. Her throat constricted, and her shoulders sagged. It was the compact. 'Tell you, Miss,' said the guard, and this time he did shake his head, 'you want to be more careful.'

*

Outside, weaving fast and blind through the moving labyrinth of shoppers, Blaithin's emotions were in riot. *Stupid, stupid, stupid, stupid.* Every step taken hard and resolute was a stricture; every dig of her nails into her palm a castigation. *Tell you Miss, you want to be more careful!* Foreign inflection. Those eyes seemed to be pursuing her along the thoroughfare. How much had they seen? It was mortifying to imagine that he...

And yet the first elation of the street's freedom refused to subside. It was caught up somehow in the giddy, terrible, impulsive thrill that had so nearly got her caught. *Stupid, stupid.* And she *was* livid with herself. She *was*. Her chest ached, her throat ached, and she knew that if she were to run now into a chance acquaintance, she'd break into uncontrollable sobs. So she pushed on, head down, colliding with passers-by, desperate to put distance between herself and the gaze she could swear she'd seen somewhere before.

Twenty minutes later, pressing her back against the door of the flat, she at last began to laugh. The *idiocy! Christ!* She began to play with the versions of the story she'd entertain Sonja with. But maybe not. Sonja might take it in the wrong spirit. She might take it badly. It had been Sonja, after all, newly returned from her sponsored hike to Machu Picchu, who'd had to pick up the pieces after the last episode, when Blaithin had been too miserable and incensed to spend Christmas with her family. It was Sonja who'd enrolled her in the gym...

She shook her head, smiling. What insane impulse had led her to drop that tiny, glittering snake into her bag? It was done before she'd time to realise it, and then those eyes in the mirror had nailed the lid shut on the act. There was no going back then.

But how much had they seen? How much did they *know*? And what was it about their mockery (was it?) that she could swear blind she'd seen somewhere before?

You're not to think about him anymore, she admonished the figure in the mirror who'd just begun to draw a bath. She'd already had one cigarette, and it vexed her that Sonja would notice the tang as soon as she got home. Because she'd be damned if she wasn't

37

going to have another, once she was underneath that rising foam, the bathroom in darkness but for a single candle. Then, at last, in water so hot it bordered on the painful, she'd luxuriate in the gorgeous terrors of what might have happened, if...

If...

Lowering herself by degrees into the exquisite torture, her skin goose-bumped and her chin bearded with foam, she heard the key grating. A girl's voice entered the flat. It made for the kitchenette, and Blaithin made out a bag of shopping and keys being set down on the counter. 'That you Sonn?' The voice went on talking. It was likely Sonja was on the mobile. Her ex-boyfriend, no doubt. Ever since Pyotr had gone back to Wroclow, they had interminable conversations.

Blaithin moved her limbs slowly so that the slow eddies wouldn't scald her. Now that Sonja was back, it'd be better not to have that cigarette. But in any case, the heat infusing her muscles was doing the job of the nicotine. So she shut her eyes, and began to imagine the shame of being dragged before the Registrar or Provost, naked as she was...

Her eyes sprang open. She'd heard a male voice. The candle was guttering. Weird shadows cavorted about the bathroom and troubled the depths of the mirror. She held her breath, and strained to hear it again. Nothing answered but the furious sputtering of the candle. 'Sonn?' The tiled bathroom retained the syllable.

Then there it was again! Low, muffled, indecipherable. *Male.* Holding herself stock still, Blaithin ran through the gamut of possibilities. All Sonja's crowd were out of the city, surely? All but what's-his-name, the lad from the gym who'd caused the flare up between Sonja and Pyotr in the first place.

So had *they* begun to go out?

Suddenly Blaithin was incensed. She had no wish for a stranger to be in the flat, not today of all days. She had no wish to be trapped in her own bathroom until such time as she heard him leave. The water was too hot. She'd had enough of it. Angrily, blindly, she patted for the Silk Cut, tapped out the last one, lifted it with her nails so as not to wet it, and held it to the candle flame. She blew copious coils of smoke into the fug. Let Sonja dare mention it! Still hunkered forward in the water, she listened. But she could hear nothing but her own vexed breathing. Had she somehow failed to hear them leave?

*

Some time later, Blaithin stepped from the bathroom's fuggy intimacy. She'd been in there so long she felt dizzy. Wrapped in a thick bath-gown and with a towel coiled turban-like, she glanced in the direction of the kitchenette. The door was shut. If they were in there, they'd been silent for an unfeasibly long time. She took a step towards her bedroom, but halted. Furious with her own timidity, she marched to the kitchen door and swung it open. The first thing she saw was Sonja, huddled over a laptop, and then the figure seated beside her.

'Oh you're home!' said her flatmate, glancing up briefly. 'Jason, Blaithin.' Then, as if an explanation might after all be required, 'Jason's helping me get Skype.'

'Blaitheyn!' Jason grinned up at her. 'I beli-*eve* we met.'

'Oh?' said Blaithin, gliding past them towards the kettle.

'I do see you down the gym an odd time.'

'Sorry,' she shrugged. She had no desire to be rude, but had no desire to make this intruder feel welcome.

'You were down in *Err*-nott's earlier Blaitheyn. Am I right?'

It was like a blow to her solar plexus. Some instinct made her shake her head, no.

'Only my mate Zbigniew said he seen you in there.'

'Zbigniew?' put in Sonja. 'Which one's Zbigniew?'

'Zbigniew! The big fella.' He winked in Blaithin's direction. 'Works as a security guard he does.'

'I don't...' Blaithin began, with admirable control of her voice. 'I don't...*know* anyone called Zbigniew.'

'All the same, he knows you. Told me he recognised you from the gym, he did.'

Blaithin again shook her head. She'd put the kettle under the tap before she realised it was already full. 'Nope, don't think so.' Then Jason stood. He took a couple of steps towards her. His faintly malevolent smirk made her shrink back. Her heart beginning to race, she watched him tender two fists towards her.

'Take your pick, Blaitheyn.'

'I'm sorry?'

'Go on! Take your pick.'

From the sofa, Sonja began to take a puzzled interest. It seemed beyond strange that Blaithin, always so feisty, should be paralysed before Jason's stupid game. But she was still as a rabbit before a cobra. 'No?' said Jason. 'Might surprise you all the same.' One of his fists opened the barest peep. Something dropped down and dangled, thin and glittering.

'Zbigniew said he seen you drop this.'

And when the girl remained mute and unmoving, he added, 'You want to be more careful Blaitheyn. You can see yourself where the catch has come loose.'

Faithful Departed

It's crazy to be cold, here. Winters in Quebec, the wind down the Lawrence would skin a mink. But here I'm cold to the bone. I dig both fists deep into my pockets and hunch my shoulders, willing the hearse on in its glacial crawl. It wouldn't do for them to see me shiver.

It's years since I've stood in Glasnevin cemetery. Dead centre of Dublin, the old joke goes. Maybe it was already a cold spot, and that's why they began to bury their dead here. Or maybe it's the sullen yews that make it cold, and infect the gravestones with lichen. All around are leprous Christs and crumbling angels. Stone too has its diseases.

Inside the church, I hadn't felt so cold. I was too busy trying not to look at Ludmilla, and my sister Kate, to have noticed. And Stevie, twisted in his wheelchair like a perpetual question mark. Or I was too busy tallying up how many of the party faithful had braved the paparazzi to pay their last respects. No former *Taoiseach*, of course. A wreath in his name took pride of place on the coffin. But the man was no fool. To be fair, there were three pews filled with apparatchiks.

A smattering has even made it to Glasnevin. They stand about in Louis Copeland coats with their aura of brandy and ruthless camaraderie. Strange as it sounds, I'm grateful to see them here.

Ciarán gave the pulpit talk. Kate's husband. By rights that task should've devolved to me. I am, after all, the eldest. But no-one had asked me, and I was hardly likely to make the suggestion myself. In fact, until the moment I mounted the rickety stairs to the airplane, it was touch and go whether I'd even make the old man's funeral.

'It'll smack of hypocrisy,' I'd reasoned. 'We'd nothing to say to one another while he was alive.'

'*Il était ton père, Jacques.*'

'He was one walking bastard, is what he was.'

'*Il était bien ton père quand même.*'

Maddy won out. I knew she would. We both did. No question of bringing the twins, though. They're too young to remember an Irish grandfather. So that meant Maddy staying behind, too. All told, the arrangement suited everybody.

My shoulder is bumped by a trench-coat and homburg, and a hand seeks out mine. 'Cold enough for ye?' Finn, Ciarán's older brother. It takes me a second to place him. He's aged. 'I tell you, Finn, I wish that bloody undertaker would find the accelerator before we all freeze to death.'

'Not as cold as Toronto, says you.'

'Quebec.'

He mouths a comic 'O'. I've always liked Finn.

'Tell us,' I say, stepping in to him, 'how've the papers treated all this…?'

He shuts one eye to find the word. 'Surprisingly *restrained*.' Over his shoulder I notice Kate is watching us. Her eyes flick away as soon as mine catch her at it. 'Give it a few days, Jack, then the gloves'll be off.'

'I won't be hanging around. I'm away first thing tomorrow.'

'Half the bloomin' country's away tomorrow.'

'So I believe. Will the last one out please turn off the lights.'

'I take it you won't be waiting around to hear the will?'

'The will, is it? The man was a bloody bankrupt!'

'Officially he was, says you! C'mere to me, what made you let that brother of mine do his speechifying in the chapel? By rights, Jack, that should've been your gig.'

'But how would the script have read then, huh? *My father spent his whole life riding the dodgems. He dodged the taxman, he dodged the financial regulator, and he dodged the party whip. He dodged the tribunals by getting cancer of the bowel. And now he's after dodging cancer by crashing the bloody limo. He'll dodge the devil yet. I'll lay even money there's nothing but stones in that coffin. Ladies and gentlemen, my father.*' Of course, I don't say a word about the years he played dodgems with my mother. But he's cute, Finn. He notices things.

'C'mere to me, your ma's not…?' He makes an open gesture towards the open grave.

'No.' A shiver runs through me. 'She's buried with her people, thank God.'

He claps his hands and rubs them as though to generate a spark. 'All the same Jacko, maybe you'd a right to say your bit about dodging the tribunals. Sure half the bloody party would've had to stand up and applaud!'

'Your brother made a fine job of the speech, Finn. I all but believed him myself!'

'Hand it to Ciarán. He'd talk for Ireland so he would.'

I look over to where Ciarán is hovering behind my sister. Tall, balding, grimly jovial. One hand is on Stevie's electric chair. 'He's a decent old skin,' I say. And as I say it, I mean it.

At last the hearse crunches to a halt and the pallbearers begin their manoeuvre. The coffin's weight seems disproportionate. When last I saw him, at Kate's wedding, my politician father was scarcely more than a scarecrow under a ridiculous wig. But in any case, everyone is watching the elegant woman dressed in black who leads her young daughter to the graveside. How grief becomes Ludmilla! The little girl's eyes are on mine, big mahogany eyes with a child's unabashed curiosity. Sophie, my half-sister. She can't have been more than three when last I saw her. I'm 'Uncle Jack', apparently, the black sheep who's too stubborn or too bloody awkward to stand with the rest of the flock. I smile at her. She doesn't smile, but she doesn't look away either.

It's far too cold for hanging about. Mercifully, even the priest thinks so. A bit of hocus-pocus, a splash of water, *in saecula saeculorum*. The cameras clack like beaks as Ludmilla lets a handful of clay dribble into the grave. Kate follows suit. Little Sophie's eyes still haven't left mine. I wink at her, shuffle forward, take up a fistful of the damp earth, crumble it and let it dance over the coffin lid. *Quand même Jacques*. He was still my father.

Kate floats over to me during the reception. Yesterday at the removal, when I'd mentioned I was only staying on a couple of days, she'd given me the frozen treatment. Now, over the effigy of a smile, she's playing reconciliatory Kate. 'How's Madeleine?'

Now, Kate had never warmed to Maddy. 'Couldn't be better. She says "hello". To Ciarán, too. And Stevie of course.'

'The twins?'

'Great. Maddy didn't think…' My hand vaguely takes in the lobby.

'Oh no. It would've been…' She shakes her hairdo to and fro. Her eyes are fluttering like butterflies from guest to guest. But her smile would sink the Titanic.

'Ludmilla looks fab.' I say this quite innocently. But as soon as

43

the words are out I'm aware of how disreputable they sound.

'It's not been easy on her.'

'No, I don't suppose it has.'

'Listen, Jack.' As she cuts to the chase, Kate's eyes semaphore to some couple or other behind my back her 'you're my *particular* friends'. Her spoken words are for my ears only. 'We could really do with you staying on a few weeks this time.'

This time? Jesus! 'But what's left to do?'

'What's left to do?' Her smile blossoms. I have to hand it to her, anyone watching would think I'd cracked the most delicious joke. 'His papers are a mess, Jack! A right bloody mess! And, and…how can you expect Ludmilla to cope with the…*gutter* press here?'

'They don't have *gutter* press on the continent?'

'So you're just going to skulk away back to Madeleine, is that it? Ok Jack. You run back to Canada. You've medals for it.'

'What would you have me do, Kate?' I can feel a strain about my mouth now. False smiles are infectious. 'It's no secret what I thought of the old bastard.'

Her eyes suddenly flash at mine. 'Mum's a long time dead, Jack. Get over it!' It's not at all what I was expecting.

'She is that!' I say, winded, and staring hard at her to figure where this sudden venom's come from. She shakes her mane magnificently as she pushes past me, and somehow it's as if the headshake sums up the collective indignation of all the assembled mourners. I'm left standing on my own. Stevie, swaying in his wheelchair, begins a low moan.

Then I spot Finn, hovering near the punchbowl, his homburg pushed comically back to entertain Sophie. So I go over.

'Here's Jack now, you can ask him yourself.'

She's giggling up at him and shaking her head 'nao!'

'Go on, ask him yourself, you don't believe me!'

'Nao! You're stupid!' she giggles, slapping his thigh.

'Ask me what?' I try.

'He says I'm a auntie,' she grins, her milk teeth missing.

'You are too!' he cries. 'You're Auntie Sophie!'

'I'm not Auntie Sophie!'

I hunker down. 'I've two little boys,' I say. 'So maybe, does that make you *Uncle* Sophie?'

She considers this for a second. She frowns up at Finn, and then grins. She shakes her ponytail, then she pushes her hot palms into my face. 'You're *stew*-pid!'

There's not much of a queue at check-in. That's one thing to be said for red-eye flights. The fluorescent strip overhead is wincing on and off, and it seems to mock my insomnia.

'Aisle or window?

'What? Oh! Whatever.'

I'm fidgety. I check my watch and consult the television screen for the umpteenth time. *Proceed to Gate*. Eyes closed, I pinch the bridge of my nose.

'Have a nice flight sir.'

'What?' Boarding card. 'Oh, thanks.'

I'd barely drifted into sleep before the four-thirty alarm call had erupted. The taxi had sped through a sleeping city. Now, everything in the great vestibule has an unreal quality to it.

Washroom.

I look at the haggard face that looks back from the mirror. Insomnia has pushed a deep thumbprint under each eye. The reflected man splashes tap-water over tired jowls, my jowls, where 'you're *stew*-pid!' her sticky hands had pressed.

The ape yawning at security barely glances at the monitor as my tray judders through. Hand-luggage and suit. Three days stay, what else are you going to need? There's a monitor high on the far wall. As I tug back on my shoes I scan it. *Boarding*. I look at my watch. Twenty minutes to take-off.

Everything in duty-free is shuttered up. A cleaner passes by with a machine that moans like a milk float. It'll be past two in the morning in Quebec. Will I manage to sleep on the flight? God I hope so!

An automated walkway trundles towards the departure gates. But I haven't stepped onto it. Instead, I'm held by a window. It's dark outside, with tiny chains of rain beading the glass. A ghost is standing at the far side, deep thumbprints of insomnia pressed beneath each eye. The ghost is watching me slip away, back to Madeleine and the twins.

A minute goes by. *His papers are a right bloody mess*. This is not my problem. The man was a gangster, pure and simple. But still the walkway trundles mechanically, loud in the building's waking vacancy. I haven't stepped onto it. Instead, I'm looking down at my hand. There's a mobile phone squatting in its palm. What the *hell* is it doing there? It'll be gone two in the morning in Quebec.

'*Maddy, c'est toi? T'ai réveillée chérie?*'

A yawn, bed-warm. What the *hell* am I doing?

'Sorry love.' I breathe out, exasperated. 'No, nothing's up. Listen. I'm going to have to stay on here a while longer. What? I don't know. A few more days. Is that ok love?'

What the *hell* am I doing? I exhale, shake my head at the character in the glass, grimace, about turn.

'You're *stew*-pid!' the hot palms had pressed into my cheeks.

Menace

The outer door is heard to clatter shut at more or less the expected time, but the small girl who comes into the kitchen is alone.

'Where's Aisling?'

The girl removes her satchel from her back and balances it, awkwardly, on a kitchen chair. Subtly, its leather strap snakes toward the side of the chair. It is as though trying to distance itself unobtrusively from the body of the satchel, but this teeters and then tumbles down onto the tiles, dragging the snaking strap after it.

As it impacts the floor, upside-down, the satchel gapes and erupts pens and school-books. Frowning after the manner of an adult, the small girl bends to gather up the spillage.

'Jessica, where's Aisling? Isn't she with you?'

The girl is looking crossly at the unhinged lid of her pencil-case and answers only by a tart swivelling of her head.

'I asked you a question young lady! Is Aisling not with you?'

The girl is still ostensibly vexed at the unhinged lid of her pencil-case, and answers in a sulk, declining to look around at the mother's voice. Her pigtails swing about with the words.

'She was meant to be with the twins!'

Crossly spoken. With reluctance, as though the girl were stating what is self-evident.

*

High heels click-clack across the porcelain surface of tiles.

'Emer! Cian!'

Instantly, through the membrane of the ceiling, the percussion of stockinged feet running across the carpeted floor. A door is heard to open, but hesitantly.

The mother waits for a moment before calling upstairs.

'Jessica says that Aisling was to come home with you two!'

The feet, unrhymed, are once again scurrying, this time as far as the head of the stairs.

'Cian, Jessica says that Aisling was to come home with you.'

She stands out into the hallway and looks upwards to where the boy is breathing in hurried spasms. Three steps higher up, the face of his twin sister, not identical, is pressed to the banister. The boy's eyes are opened into two globes.

'She was, – with Una, – Mahaffy!'

The voice is uneven because her son is asthmatic. His eyes dilate a fraction more, and he adds, 'She was, – never supposed to, – come home with us!'

'Did she *say* she was going home with Una Mahaffy? Did you *ask* her was she going home with her?'

'I...'

The head swivels about towards that of the twin sister, then back through the banisters. The eyes are still opened preternaturally wide.

'She was playing with her. With Una Mahaffy.' And with creased forehead he clarifies '– in the yard.'

'Yes, but did you talk to her? Did you ask her?'

*

'Hello? Hello, Rita?'

'–'

'This is Julie Quigly.'

'–'

'Yes, listen, Rita. I was just wondering, has Una come in yet?'

'–'

'I see.'

'–'

'No, no!'

'–'

'Not at all! Listen, Rita? I was wondering, could you do me a small favour?'

'–'

'Yes. Could you just give me a ring as soon as Una gets in, that's all?'

'–'

'Oh, no! Nothing like that!'

'–'

'You're sure you don't mind?'

48

'_'

'Listen, thanks a million. Goodbye, now.'

'_'

'Thanks, Rita. Bye.'

*

The phone is watching. It is coiled. It is waiting to be sprung by the return call.

And in the interim a fistful of dough is pulled out of a mixing bowl and squeezed tightly. The woman's fingers have been dampened in another bowl, this one filled with water the surface of which trembles at her every movement. Behind the two bowls, not entirely obscured, sleeps a kitchen knife.

When the ball of dough is worked and compressed she slaps it onto a flour-whitened board. It is rolled, flattened out. The pastry is pummelled, rolled again, lifted, laid over the surface of a casserole, tucked in at the edges. Then the woman sprinkles a very slight snow of flour, and with a metal fork she sets tracks that are not unlike the print of some winter bird into the floured surface.

But all this is mechanical.

The eye is fixed on the silence of the phone that clings onto the wall.

*

Now her hand, fingers still whitened, hovers uneasily in the vicinity of the bone-coloured receiver. Is it too soon to call again?

But all at once the telephone erupts into shrill alarm. The trill, nervous, sounds upwards into the air like a dangerous insect. A second trill almost has time to rise after it.

'Hello, yes?'

'_'

'It's me!'

'_'

'I see. Just now. And, ehm, Rita? I was wondering, Aisling isn't with her?'

'_'

'No, no!'

'_'

'Not at all, no. Nothing to be alarmed...'

'_'

'No. It's just that Cian said that he'd seen them together.'

'_'

'Yes, if you don't mind. Thanks, Rita. I'll hang on…'

*

There is silence gathering upstairs, a weighty silence, unbroken except for the sound of a cistern filling, this and the faint, sharply regular breath through the banisters.

She has cradled the receiver between ear and neck and is rooting through her handbag. Three fine white streaks of flour scathe its leather body.

She is trying to locate a small pocket address book. She is trying to interpret the tiny sounds that she might discern at the other end of the telephone.

'_'

'Yes? Hello.'

'_'

'I see. She didn't...?'

'_'

'No, not at all. No.'

'_'

'Yes. I'm sure that's it.'

'_'

'That must be it. Listen, thanks a million, Rita.'

'_'

'No, I'm sure...'

'_'

'I will, of course!'

'_'

'Bye now. Bye.'

*

Outside and under the vast evening.

The air is cooling. The air is losing its light.

'Cian. Run over to Melissa O'Byrne and ask her if she's seen Aisling. Hurry on, now.'

'Emer. You mind Jessica. That's a good girl.' And to answer the searching eyes, 'I'll be back in a minute.'

An afterthought.

'Emer!'

Eyes shut, open. Calmly, for the love of God!

'Emer, don't answer the door. Not unless you know who it is. Sure you won't love?'

*

The grasses are tossing about like the mane of some hunkered animal. There is an edge to the wind.

'AISLING!'

The light has thinned out still further. The sky has become a silver foil, luminous through the leafless twigs of the hedge.

At the second gate a blackbird, startled, threads through the evening brambles with gurgling alarm call.

'AISLING!'

Numb silence of the fields.

'AISLING!'

And the child's voice at her waist:

'Ais-ling!'

*

A pair of car's headlights whiten the hedgerow into a petrified arc and then strike blindly across them. A gravel sound, the wheels shirking to a halt.

Then it seems a mask-like face is instantaneously straining out of the opened window, craning right at them, a face like a child's caricature of Melissa O' Byrne.

'Julie I heard! Have you tried the school?'

Crimson lipstick and dark lines of mascara behind the horn-rimmed glasses, a grotesque parody so poor is the light.

'The school?'

'You'd never know. She might have stayed behind with one of the teachers.'

No! No!

'But surely they would have rung me to say so!'

'But it's worth a try Julie. Do you not think? If only so as to find out who she was with before she left.'

The hesitation. The worried glance along the ditch, along the field.

'Come on! It won't take five minutes to drive down as far as the school. You must be frozen out there, the pair of you.'

Her own hesitation is agony to her.

'No, I...'

'But at the school at least you'll be able to ask them! Do you not think? And if they don't know anything, then at least they'll be able to come on out here and help you look.'

'I...'

A last glance back toward the fields. Melissa O' Byrne's hand is already opening the car-door for them.

*

Now it is all but dark.

A single star, bright, low to the west. A thin moon, like a shaving taken from a thumbnail.

The wind has a keen edge to it by this time. It wrinkles the surface water that lies in flat pools to the sides of the fields. It tosses the tufts of greyed grasses. It sifts the hawthorn hedges.

'AISLING!'

All across the fields fingers of light stretch out from restless hand-torches.

'AISLING!'

Her child's name echoes about the twilight, across this field, across the next. It echoes as far as the canal. In various pitches. In unknown voices.

Fingers of white light probe among the roots, probe along the ditchwater. In their livid circles of light, the jagged edges of cans take on the proportions of a disaster.

'AISLING!'

A black rag of plastic fluttering, caught on a barb of wire. A bird, erupting from its nest.

*

Then, once only but prolonged, there sounds the brittle pitch of a referee's whistle. It is somewhere over to the left. It is uncomfortably shrill.

The whistle is shrill as the needle that is cocked next to a balloon.

Little Hamlet

Larry Fenton is the boy next door. He's in my class. Now that he's gone to summer school there's nothing to do around here. But when *He* said I had to go to summer school, I screamed at them that I wouldn't go.

When the bus was three miles outside town, I had a fit. If you hold your breath for long enough that you see flashes all around your eyes, sometimes it works. And then I knew the busman wouldn't be able to find my atomiser, because I'd hidden it underneath the seat when Mrs Hughes wasn't looking. So after that I didn't have to go to summer school.

When we were back in the house after my dad's funeral, Fr Dolan put his hand on my head. He has huge big hands, as big as two coal shovels and just as black Mr Fenton says. He's Larry's dad. He's a joker. He always winks at you when he makes a joke.

So Fr Dolan put his hand on my head after we got back from the funeral and he said 'You're the man of the house now.'

Mummy cried when she heard him say it.

I used to read to Mummy back then. Or sometimes she used to read to me. On Sunday morning, which was her day off, we used to read together. Sunday was her day off before *He* came to live with us. Back then Mummy used to let me climb into her bed, and then we'd read. Sometimes it was a schoolbook. Sometimes it was stories from the paper.

She wouldn't ever let me have breakfast in her bed because she said I'd only fill it with crumbs.

But then when I went in one day, afterwards, and Mummy was sitting back in the bed with her hair down and spread all about the pillow, *He* shouted at me to get out. He was standing at the wardrobe. Later on she came into my room and said that I was gone too big to get into bed and read to her anymore. She asked me to stop crying. I always cry when I'm angry and I hate it because only little boys are supposed to cry. But I was crying and then I tried to slap her and then she had to hold my wrists very hard so that it hurt. She made a face at me and said I was bad but

I didn't tell her the real reason, which is that I was angry not because of what *He* said, that I couldn't come into the room and everything, but because when he said it I saw Mummy smiling. Mummy never has her hair down like that, and I saw her smiling, but she didn't think that I'd seen it. It wasn't a real smile, it was sad, but still it was a smile all the same.

And now even when I have nightmares about my dad still I'm not allowed to go into Mummy's room anymore. I hate him. He's changed everything.

Mummy explained to me that we were very poor. She said that the suit that I wore to the funeral cost her three weeks' wages and that it would have to do. Even though I'd grown since then and now it was gone too small for me. She said she could let down the legs a little bit and let out the waist. But even so it was still too small for me and anyway I didn't even want to be there at the church, with everyone looking. No way.

So then the day before the wedding I said to Larry Fenton that we'd play down at the old house. Afterwards, I had to stay with the Fentons, when they went away to the hotel on their honeymoon. I suppose it's ok staying with the Fentons because Mr Fenton is funny, but it's not so great when Orla is there. She's Larry's sister, and Mr Fenton pretends that we're sweethearts. But he only does it to get on my nerves. She's only six, and whenever we go out to play, she has to play too.

But then when Larry comes over to my house to play or when we meet down in the old house or in the bottom field, then she doesn't have to come and play.

The old house is a wreck. Mr Fenton said it's haunted, but he was only messing. I saw him wink at Mrs Fenton when he said that.

So when I met Larry Fenton down in the bottom field the day before the wedding he said I must be totally bonkers. He said I must be mad, to be wearing my suit and everything.

The house is a real wreck. It's all full of cobwebs and dust and every single window has been broken. There was even a fire in one end and you can see the sky when you look up through the roof. The room where the fire was smells like piss. I think it was the kitchen or something.

At the other end of the house there's this sort of a pit. That's where we sometimes play. It's overgrown with weeds and nettles and sometimes you can even see rats down there. But he said I must be totally bonkers because when they saw the cut of my suit they'd kill me. But I didn't care. I even jumped into the pit and rolled around in it on purpose. I started to wrestle Larry Fenton, and at first he didn't want to, but then he sort of got angry. There's all sorts of rubbish and muck in the pit, but I rolled around in it all the same and when we were wrestling he pushed my face in the dirt too.

And then when we went climbing through the attic, I caught my shoulder on a nail and the suit got torn. Just a little tear, but that was by accident. Even though they didn't believe me, that tear was by accident. Mummy was crying and saying that I did it on purpose after all the money she'd had to save and that I was a bad son to her and that's why I was crying too. It was *not* because *He* had taken off his belt and was going to strap me. And later on in my room when he put me over the chair and started to strap me I was nearly choking. I knew *He* wasn't going to stop until he made me cry and I tried so hard not to that I was choking. There was this huge big knot in my throat and my eyes were scalding hot. And then I started having this fit where I couldn't breathe. It felt like I was drowning but still I couldn't breathe and then he got real scared and he had to call Mummy in.

That's when I decided to learn the trick. Now sometimes I can make myself have a fit, just by holding my breath and rolling my eyes.

And then one day when they were away on the honeymoon Larry Fenton showed me where Mr Fenton keeps the rat poison. It's in a box marked with a skull and crossbones. That's because it could kill you, if you swallowed it by accident or anything. He told me it was very dangerous, that even if you only took just a tiny bit of it like just half a spoonful or so that still you could go blind or something. I said I didn't believe him but he swore it was true.

So then later he said if I didn't believe him, we could try it out on the dog that's chained to the gate up at McGowen's. That was Larry Fenton's idea, to try it out on McGowen's dog. It's vicious.

Mummy says it's a disgrace, the way the McGowens keep their animals. The dog is always barking and chasing after you. If it ever managed to slip out of its chain it could eat you alive. But then Larry Fenton had to go to summer camp so we never got round to it.

The day after I had the fit on the bus, *He* said that I'd have to go and see a specialist. He said how he has a sister up in Dublin and she's a nurse or something and that I could go and stay with her. He said the change would do me good.

He didn't say any of this when I was there. I was supposed to be outside playing with the twins. Sometimes Mrs O' Grady leaves the twins for the whole day in our house and then I'm supposed to play with them. They're ok I suppose but I didn't want to play sticky toffee and that's what the twins always want to play. So then we were near the window and that's when I could hear *Him* telling mummy about it. How he was going to send me away, and then I'd have to stay with his stupid sister up in Dublin.

Mummy didn't say anything.

I didn't sleep at all, not for the whole night. I kept thinking how *He* was going to send me away. And Mummy didn't say anything. That meant that even if she was sad about it he was still going to get his way. I kept thinking about how I hate him, and how I'd hate to have to live up in Dublin with his stupid sister. I even thought about what Fr Dolan said after the funeral that I was the man of the house now.

I kept thinking all that day and night and I didn't get any sleep. I kept thinking about it all the next day too. It took me absolutely ages to come up with a plan though. But then at tea-time I saw that Mummy had made a meat-loaf because that's *His* favourite, and that's when I thought of the plan.

So the night before yesterday when everyone was in bed asleep I sneaked out of my room and I went to the kitchen with the torch that Mr Fenton gave me for Christmas. Mr Fenton said that it wasn't from him it was from my sweetheart. He's always messing that Orla Fenton is supposed to be my sweetheart. Sometimes I use it to read under the covers at night and when you hold it against the skin of your hand you can sort of see the bones underneath.

When I got to the kitchen I opened the drawer and I took out the big carving-knife. I'm not supposed to go near the knife drawer but I was careful not to touch the blades or anything. Then when I got the knife I went to where Mummy keeps the meat-loaf. She always puts it near the window under a tea-towel. That's to keep away the flies in the summer. Then I cut a slice.

I knew *He* was asleep because I could hear him snoring, so then I went to the door and put it on the latch and then I pulled it shut after me, but I didn't shut it properly because I don't have a key to get back in. I didn't even need the torch outside because the moon was so big and bright. Except when I got inside Mr Fenton's tool shed. Then I needed the torch all right. It was sort of scary, being in there on my own at night and it was really dark, and when you shine a torch on something it kind of looks like it's waiting to move or to attack you or something like that.

My hand was shaking when I found the box of rat poison. And then what made things worse is that it was opened sort of with a tear and when I dropped it it spilled all over the place. But in the end I managed to spoon it back up with the plastic spoon out of the box and I covered the slice of meat-loaf in it too and then I swept the floor and the shelf to make sure that there was no more of it lying around. I kept thinking that even if it didn't work that at least there'd be enough to make him real sick, and then I'd have to stay at home with Mummy.

But then when I was walking back to the house over the field I sort of began to think that maybe it wasn't such a good idea. Maybe *He* would notice, or maybe Larry Fenton was wrong and you'd need absolutely loads of it to poison anyone. And then I thought anyway he still hadn't given his sister the phone call about me having to go up and stay with her and maybe Mummy would make him change his mind.

So in the end I decided to try it out on the dog instead.

McGowen's is up on the other side of the hill but it's not too far away if you take the shortcut. When I got near to the gate the moon came out and then I could see that the dog was still chained to the gate but that he was asleep. I was sort of scared that he'd wake up. He's really vicious and everything and anyway if he started barking then he'd probably wake up the whole house. But when I had nearly sneaked up on him I think he must have growled or something and then I threw him the bit of meat-loaf and it landed pretty near him. At first he didn't seem to notice it though. He was growling like under his breath and I sneaked away backwards but I don't think he'd even seen me. No way.

Then I had to wait for ages before he got up and walked over to the bit of meat-loaf. I waited so long on my hunkers that I had a cramp in my leg. But he just sniffed at the bit of meat-loaf and then he turned around and lay back down again.

Later on he must have eaten it all the same. At about two in the morning you could hear this sort of howling. It was really creepy. It was like a howl or a yelp or something, and then you'd hear nothing. Then maybe a half hour later you'd hear him howling again. He must have really been in agony. And the next day when we saw Mrs McGowen at mass she told Mummy that when Mr McGowen went out to go down for the paper he was already dead.

Anyway at least now I know that it works. If *He* thinks that he's going to send me away to live with his stupid sister up in Dublin he just better watch it, that's all.

The Arithmetic of Chance

My father's uncle held up his wineglass and for some time appeared to be considering how it gathered the fading light. 'I'll tell you all about the arithmetic of chance,' he declared at length. This was unusual. Captain Ned, as we called him, was the quiet one of the family. It was Billy who was the talker. But that Christmas, 'Uncle' Billy was in hospital. I saw at once that Captain Ned had the undivided attention of the entire table, and although I was scarcely seven years of age and was more than fond of plum pudding in brandy sauce, I laid down my spoon.

'You know the pig-farm over the far side of the Abbey Bridge?' Captain Ned inquired of my father.

'The McCabe farm, is it?'

'The McCabe farm. But do you know how it came to be the McCabe farm?'

Father shook his head and exchanged a quick glance with Kathleen, who was six years older than I. It was as much as to say 'the very farm you were asking me about Kitty!' Then he fired me a wink and wrinkled up his nose, because everyone knows a pig-farm is stinky.

'I'll tell you,' continued my granduncle. 'At that time, by which time I mean in the run up to the Great War, that farm belonged to old Jack Kiely. Now Kiely had two sons, two fine strapping twins by the name of Dónal and Seán. Their mother Annie had died of the puerperal fever as soon as ever she was delivered of them, leaving himself a widower of fifty-five. Whether it was on account of the pigs or on account of his years, old Jack Kiely never looked to wed again.

'Now that was all right. All along, it was understood that when the time came, the farm would devolve to Dónal, who was the older of the two by a matter of ten or fifteen minutes. Whether Seán was destined for the priesthood or for the emigration ship was a decision that could be put off until the lad reached his majority. There was a girl, too, a lass by the name of Bridget, though she was only their cousin, or half-cousin maybe. She was what they used call a love child. The way it was told to me, the girl's mother, who was the wild sister of the late Annie Kiely, had fled to England in disgrace as soon as ever her confinement was up. So it was left to old Jack Kiely to raise the child along with his own.

'Now that was all very well. The seasons turned as is their way, and the twins grew strong and fearless and were soon the holy terror of anyone had to take on our local football club. Seán in particular could field a ball over any lad had three inches on him, and by Christ he wasn't afraid to use the elbow either! Dónal was the more dependable maybe, but 'twas Seán had the wicked sense of humour that was every bit as admired and feared as was his famous elbow. It was at that time I first got to know them. They'd been through the mangle of a Christian Brothers' education, and like so many young guns at that time, they weren't averse to playing at boy scouts up the back hills with the Volunteers. Not that you'd ever hear so much as a political opinion out of ere a one of them. If they couldn't see it or hold it in their hands, they'd no interest in it.

'So that was all right. Then, in nineteen hundred and thirteen, I got my commission, and so that was the end of that. There was no more Gaelic football for Neddy boy! Our paths diverged after, and I knew no more of their story until we met again,' he paused, 'unexpectedly.' Mother had come in with a lamp from the kitchen, and while she put a match to it Uncle Ned filled his pipe and then lit up with a reed he held into the lamp's chimney. ''Twas in France,' he added, puffing out a curl of thick, yellow smoke. The room began to take on a sweet nut smell. I thought how it would've been lovelier without the lamp, watching the pipe glow red each time he drew on it.

'Now this much of the story I have on good authority, because Fr Dineen showed it to me in the parish records. Young Bridget Kiely – in the absence of a father they had to give her some class of a name I suppose – had been born in the same year as the new century. And all the while the boys were fighting and farming and growing up into the two finest swearers and swaggerers that ever terrorised the parish, she was developing into the sullen, silent type. Hair the colour of a sorrel mare tossing her mane in the dawn, and eyes! Eyes on her that smouldered like that there briar.' He held aloft his pipe. 'Do you mind her Francie?'

'I heard talk of her,' sighed my father. 'I never met her.'

'It's a pity,' mused my granduncle, angling his glass to catch the glow of the oil lamp while he waved the pipe so that its smoke curled around it. I had the queer idea he was trying to give a notion of the girl's mane of hair. 'She'd have served famously for one of your blessed ballads Francie!' he laughed. In those days, Father was something of a balladeer, popular at wakes and weddings.

"Faith, Ned, maybe it's yourself should be writing the ballads!' put in Mother from the corner. 'A sorrel mare tossing her mane in the dawn, says you!'

'Ah Pegeen, if you'd seen her in those days!' Captain Ned shook his head and clenched the pipe between his back teeth. When he had it glowing again, he went on. 'For the next part of my story, I'm indebted to Corporal Jimmy Foley. Now Foley was charged with accompanying the recruiting sergeant around the three counties whenever they'd sunk the Lusitania, back in fifteen. There was some class of a fair on here in the town that day, and towards the close of it, the bold sergeant had set out his stall outside of Slattery's Public House. Posters of Kirchner and Redmond and "Avenge the Lusitania. Join an Irish Regiment Today."' Suddenly, Captain Ned fixed a fierce eye on mine. 'Nigh on a quarter of a million answered that call, boy.' He set down his glass with a thump and pointed a long finger. 'Whatever else they may tell you in your school, you must never forget that. By Christ, when I think of the way…'

'Go on with your story, Edward,' growled Father, his palm open.

'Very good.' The old man drew deep on the pipe, and a wreath of smoke rose towards the ceiling. 'The corporal,' he winked at me, 'who was a wee scaltán of a buck from up beyond Clonmel, knew all about the Kiely twins on account of their fearsome reputation on the football pitch. He also knew that they were about as like to take the King's shilling as Fr Dineen or Sr Mary Aloysius! So that was all very well. But the next thing, just as they're about to shut up shop, having signed up none but the Pisser Flynn, there's all sorts of rows and ructions and up strides Seán Kiely, with the brother hanging out of him.

'You'll not do it so long as there's a breath of life left in me,' cries Dónal.

'Get off of me, or by Christ I'll leave you gasping for that breath of life,' growls Seán, and by the thunder in his brow there was none thought he was making one of his jokes. 'By Jesus I'll stretch you if you don't leave go of my arm.'

'The recruiting sergeant of course winks at Jimmy Foley, as much as to say hold on there now, maybe we'll have a look see what way the wind is blowing here. And a great crowd is beginning to gather round and they jostling and nudging to see what was going to come of it all. No prizes, Francie, for guessing what it was all about. Twenty years before, chance had seen to it that Dónal had been the first out of the womb, and with it, he'd a right to inherit the pig-farm whenever old Jack Kiely passed on. But then, by way of compensation maybe, chance had given the younger twin the quick wit and the cheeky smile, and he was ever the more popular of the two. So that it's no surprise maybe which one of the brothers the lass was drawn to, and she developing into a sullen, smouldering kind of a beauty that had the pair of them driven mad as two young bulls. You could've scripted it!

'This is not our fight,' cries Dónal, pulling back the other by the shoulders and staring daggers at the recruiting sergeant.

'No it is not!' And Seánín shakes himself free and waves a huge fist under his brother's nose. 'You know well where our fight is Dónal Kiely!' Then he draws himself up with a swagger. 'And if you were half the man I took you to be, you'd sign up too, and let whoever comes back take all.' Then the pair of them square up to one another eye to eye and as Jimmy Foley put it, it was that tense, you would've been scared stiff to let a pin drop.

'Now this was the first real inkling that any of us had that all was not well out on the pig-farm. The girl, you must remember, was only after entering her fifteenth year and besides the fact you couldn't get the time of day out of her, wasn't she their half-sister or their cousin or something? It came out afterwards of course that she used to go walking with Seán Kiely of an evening, and that the brother Dónal was racked with a *grá* for her. But if it was the joker she showed a preference for, what sort of a future could Seán Kiely offer the girl, and he destined for the army or the emigrant boat?

'All right,' says Dónal, his own fist clenched every bit as tight as his brother's, 'all right. Show us that ledger there,' says he, and in the heel of the hunt, didn't the pair of them sign up there and then on that black fair-day, leaving none but the girl and the old man to look after the pig-farm for who knew how long. What they couldn't sort out between them, blind chance would have to sort out on the battlefields of Flanders.'

In the corner, my mother tut-tutted.

'That night, I needn't tell you Pegeen, all hell broke loose back on the farm. Old Jack was well into his seventies and looking to pass the running of the place onto younger shoulders. As for the lass, we can only imagine the state she was thrown into by this sudden caprice. But there was no reasoning with the boys, not once they'd given their word, and in public. You'd have to feel for young Bridget, though. Once the old man got wind of the fact that she was part way responsible for the disaster, he made her life so miserable out there that she'd have upped sticks and left for the city if it wasn't for the fact that the old man's health was failing. He came to depend on her those last months, but by all accounts, what with his jibes and jeers and her silences, it can't've been an easy existence on e'er a one of them.

'It was in the build-up to the big summer push that I crossed paths with the Kiely twins again. Different company of course, but my own regiment. Pals regiments, that's the British way.' He pointed the stem of his pipe at Father. 'That's the principle on which they run half the world Francie.'

'Is it?' said Father, letting on to be uninterested. 'Good luck to them.'

'Now, by this stage in the proceedings, I'd already had a brace of horses shot out from under me. Seen dozens of Irish lads sent home in boxes, too, or worse. There was no need to tell me all about the arithmetic of chance. It wasn't always the brave or the foolhardy either. What you soon come to realise is, a whiz-bang or a bullet knows nothing about how brave or how cowardly a man might be. A bomb is every bit as blind as the blindest lottery. Oh, sometimes you fancy you can see when a fella's number is up. He looks paler, maybe, or there's an aura about him. Or he doesn't seem to be entirely present, as if a part of him has already crossed over into the realm of shadows. I don't know. So much superstition, probably. But still…' Captain Ned's pipe had gone out. At this point he tapped out the ash onto the side-plate, slowly, as though he were thinking about something. He took a plug of tobacco from his pocket and began to scrape shavings from it with a pocketknife. I looked from my father to my sister Kitty, to see if either of them was going to ask him to go on with his story. Finally, it was Mother who broke the spell. 'Well, Ned, and what became of the boys?'

'What became of the boys?' His thumb pushed the flakes of tobacco into the bowl of his briar, and he lit another reed from the oil lamp. He sucked on it and puffed several times and then clenched the pipe in his back teeth. 'What became of the boys was this. The boys, as you rightly call them Pegeen, appeared to be leading a charmed life altogether. In one attack after another, half of the platoon might be done for, but not my bold Kielys. I'm told they were past courageous. But maybe it's not the word. It was more that they showed an absolute disdain in the teeth of danger. They never forgot, d'you see, what it was that they were looking for, so far from home. But it'd take a wiser man than me to distinguish between that class of disdain and true bravery. It wasn't long before it was noticed what's more. They were decorated. And such was the rate of attrition in the regiment that summer that it wasn't long before Dónal was made corporal, and then sergeant a bare two month after that, and I daresay Seán would've followed him up through the ranks if it wasn't for the mouth he had on him.

'A year went by. Word came that their old man wasn't long for the world. The truth is, he'd been in decline ever since the day his two fine sons took the King's shilling. It so fell out that this news arrived during a lull in the fighting, when the regiment was several miles back from the front and in the process of being brought back up to strength. So there'd have been no great difficulty in securing compassionate leave. But the two boys wouldn't do it. They'd made a compact with chance, d'you see, and chance would have to sort out which of them was to get the prize. So the old man died alone and embittered, unmourned by any of his own but the young girl he'd raised and had come to blame. It was at that time that McCabe was seen about the place. Sure someone had to look after the business until such time as the boys came home.'

'How was that possible Ned?' interrupted Father. 'What sort of a claim did McCabe have on the place?'

65

'None that I'm aware of Francie. He was a journeyman worked in the piggery, is all. Played at the Volunteers at the time the two boys used to go out, so maybe it was Dónal gave him the nod to look after the place. It was a strategic interest you must remember. You wouldn't be allowed let it to go to wrack and ruin at a time when the entirety of Britannia was on half-rations. And then, the old man was no fool. He wasn't the type to let his life's work fall apart on account of his two boys were run amuck, so maybe his hand was behind it.'

'So then, it was this McCabe lad that Bridget fell for, is that it?' asked my mother from the shadows.

'Not at all! Would you wait till I finish girl! The more the fighting wore on, the more reckless the two boys became. Their bravado was fast becoming the stuff of song and legend. But there's only so long you can thumb your nose at Fate, I suppose. It was at the time of the last big German push, just before the Americans began to arrive over by the boatful. Life had never been so precious as that spring, for the word in the trenches was if you could only hang on now, the war would end and you'd be home to a hero's welcome. It was then they picked to push their luck once too often. 'Twas Seán Kiely, of course. He'd volunteered for some madcap piece of reconnoitring one dark night towards the end of March. I mind there was a thin sly grin of a moon hanging about three hours above the sunset, over to the west. Once it went down, it was dark enough to set out on a belly crawl. But whatever way the ground had shifted in the run up to that night, it was all uncharted terrain, and halfway into no man's land, didn't he trigger a mine that took off the half of his leg.

'He did his best to stifle all cries and pants, for he knew well his brother wasn't the man to leave him out there to bleed to death if he knew he was still alive. And sure enough, within the half-hour, Sgt Dónal had crawled out as far as him against all advice, order and imprecation. He tied a makeshift tourniquet to stop the bleeding and, crater by crater, he dodged the marksmen and the flares to haul the brother back to friendly lines. 'Christ, why couldn't you leave me to die?' cries Seán as they tied him into the stretcher, and he hitting out at everyone left, right and centre. 'What use am I to anyone as half of a man?'

'But he was wrong. In fact, he went a long way to making a remarkable recovery. All that autumn, once he'd been discharged from the veteran's hospital, you'd see him hopping about the place on the crutches or on the wooden leg, bossing the school kids around at the harvest, chasing the girls and generally making things difficult for McCabe where the young Bridget was concerned. Not wooing her on his own account, mind. He'd got it into his head that his brother had won their infernal bet, and now it was up to him to safeguard the prize until such time as the Sergeant was demobbed.

'But he'd counted without chance. You don't challenge Fate, and then walk away from the game.' Captain Ned stuck the reed a third time into the chimney of the lamp and then drew on his pipe until once more it glowed a cherry red in the dark room. 'A bare fortnight before the guns fell silent for once and for all, a wet Halloween it was, didn't a stray bullet accidentally discharged lodge itself into Dónal Kiely's temple and he two mile from the front line. Stone dead before ever he knew what hit him. That bullet,' he went on, pointing the stem of the briar at Father, 'did more to take the heart out of Seán Kiely than a German mine ever could. He sort of gave up after that. No more you'd see him, hopping about the place and taking the rise out of the cailíní. No more, shepherding young Bridget away from the wiles of young McCabe from the piggery. In fact, in the heel of the hunt, didn't he sign over the whole business to Bridget, and he disappeared into one of them bungalows was built for the war cripples out on the Cork road. He was never much heard of after that.'

The room fell silent. I could make out the gurgle of smoke sputtering up the chimney of the lamp.

'And so Bridget married the McCabe character?' asked my mother.

'And so, eventually, Bridget married the McCabe character,' said my granduncle, and then he looked at my sister Kitty, 'and that is how the pig-farm became the McCabe farm.'

Mother tut-tutted. Then silence again fell over the room. I picked up my spoon, but the plum-pudding was cold and stodgy.

'And that, Francie,' added my granduncle at length, drawing the last heat from his dying briar, 'is the arithmetic of chance.'

Ghost Estate

All that summer, we hung out round the back of the estate. The Ma said to keep the hell out of it, that there was all sorts of traps and dangers in there. One of the Brennans, Peter I think it was, had stood on a plank with this six-inch nail sticking out of it that'd gone all the way through his shoe and up through his foot so it had. And then he got septicaemia out of it and he was lucky not to lose the foot. Or so the Ma said anyhow. You never knew but. Ma was always telling stories.

You didn't hang around the estate, where the Jaysus were you supposed to hang out but? It wasn't like when we lived in Dublin. I was only young but I still remember. And now the pavees was after making camp along the canal and you didn't want to be messing with pavees. Josser Kelly seen them kicking fair shite out of a couple of seniors the night of the GAA do, so it wasn't like we were going to hang out down there any more. Chances are it would've been ok most of the time, but you never knew with pavees and anyway we were getting too old to go messing jumping off of the bridge in our cacks. Besides the fact it was starting to look like a tip so it was, like we were still living in Finglas West. What the Da does call the God's own country but Ma says is the back of beyonds.

The first few months when there'd been machinery and everything still lying around, there used to be this security guard was always knocking about. Big fucker in a blue uniform with a baldy head on him and an Alsatian dog. Polish I think he was. But then once they'd took the machinery away he sort of disappeared too. Nothing left to feck says you. Then there was only this wire fence around the place with signs to keep out but it was dead easy crawl under that once you knew where the gaps was. That was last February.

The estate being well off the main road there was plenty of places you wouldn't be seen. Even if you'd a bonfire going, there was certain places was well hid from the road. There was two rows of half-finished houses built out of breeze blocks with black plastic still sticking out, and then behind them entire rows of nothing but foundations, one after another like concrete scabs and pipes sticking up out of them you could drop stones into and listen for the plop. The whole place was all full of planks and broken pipes and rusty wire and nettles and puddles of cement gone hard and this scabby concrete mixer on its side so the Ma wasn't too far wrong, it was dead easy get a scrape or a twisted ankle so it was. But if you wanted to have a smoke or something, or say if you were copping a feel off of one of the twins, there was no shortage of corners where you wouldn't be seen. Anyhow, it was somewhere to hang out.

The only house none of us dared go into was the one at the end. That was the nearest to being finished, with planks crossways in the roof where the slates were supposed to go and even a few windows with tape on them, though most of them was well broke by now. I think it was supposed to be the show house if ever it got finished. Big fucking if.

That was the house where they found Mr McHugh, the week before the Christmas holliers. His car, a big Merc it was, had been sitting outside that house for days on end before they found him. McHugh Construction. Or no, it's the developer he was by that stage. He used to be a builder, but. It was said round town he'd falsified accounts or something. Ma said it was a pity about him, but Da said he wasn't the worst of them, not by a long chalk. Besides the fact it was bad luck to speak ill of the dead. That was the Da all over.

Jacinta McHugh used to be in my year but she was took out and kept home after they found her old man dangling from the rafters. The head come into geography class and whispered something real quiet to Ginger Lynch, and then he took Jacinta out dead gentle, like he was apologising for something. I'll always remember that. The younger brother Shane was still in Brigid's at the time, the kid who went missing later on. He was chubby, like his sister, and the same squinty eyes on him. So none of us would go into that end house, not on our own anyhow, and never once it got dark. Bucko had brought a mot in there one night and something had happened had scared the pair of them shitless. Normally you wouldn't believe the Hail Mary out of Bucko's mouth, but the state he was in, it made you think. And there was a couple of queer stories doing the rounds in town, so like I say, by and large we steered clear of the gaff. It got so it was a kind of a dare with us.

The best thing was, you weren't much bothered by anyone once you were inside that fence. An odd time you'd come across courting couples or you'd find a needle to say some junkie'd been shooting up, but the older lads from the town never seemed to bother with the place. All of which was class because it meant we could use the shed as a stash, to lay up cans or bottles of cider a night something was planned. The padlock was busted but we used to sort of close it over to let on it was locked. You could shut someone inside all right, if you were messing with them, but you couldn't stop someone from the outside getting in. So as long as no one was hanging round the gaff, that was grand.

That year we were to go into transition year, so you could say we were a pretty innocent bunch. We'd all got the wear out of the twins, and Josser Kelly said he'd gone the whole hog with Annie Ward. She's the town skank. Maybe he had and all. But one thing's for sure, we all of us had the serious hots for Lua Cavanagh, who was sort of the opposite of Annie Ward when it came to that kind of thing. She was after growing about six inches since the previous year, you want to have seen the legs on her, and all that summer she wore these hot pants that, I swear to Jaysus...

So August was getting on, and there was only just over a week left till we were all back in school and that's when Shane McHugh went missing. The whole town was out looking for him on account of the sister Jacinta was on tranquillisers and anti-depressants and all. I mean she was only our age for fuck sake. Even the families that'd been ruined by McHugh was prepared to help the search. To give an idea of how bitter things had got, these were the very ones had keyed his Merc and sprayed graffiti on the walls of his premises in the run up to the night they found him, and even then, there was some like Josser's Uncle Dave who'd lost everything that'd sooner cross the street than say hello to the widow. Ma always said Da had a right to be more angry seeing how it was on the strength of McHugh Construction that we'd made the move down here in the first place, and now she said we'd debts we'd never pay off. That was all forgotten for these few days of the search, but. So these pictures of Shane McHugh in his confirmation suit started going up all over town and the Garda frogmen went diving the length and breadth of the canal, but after three days there was still no sign of him. It was on the national news, too, on account of McHugh Construction and the suicide and everything.

Now that was all well and good, but it made the Ma even more wary about me going into the estate. As if Shane McHugh had fell down one of the pipes for fuck sake! They'd even scoured the place for him the very first day. Still, as Da would wink at me, there's women's logic for you! The problem of course being that we had this one last big blow-out planned for midnight on the Friday, seeing as how the following Tuesday we were all back in school. Ma must've got wind of it too coz she was adamant I was going nowhere that night so she was, not with the Da still out helping with the search and everything. So the net result was that I'd to sneak out of the gaff by dropping out the window at half eleven at night after I heard the Ma turning out the telly in her bedroom.

There was already a bonfire lit by the time I got there, and everyone was lying about it and they half blotto so they were. I done a few quick shots to try and catch up, in particular because Lua Cavanagh was there that night and once or twice I caught her looking at me. She had this braid done into her hair that fell down over her forehead and had beads on the end of it, dead sexy it was. Of course Bucko was already puking his ring up over by the cement mixer. I swear, I don't know why he bothers his arse drinking.

So to cut a long story short, after I was there about an hour we started getting to play this spin the bottle game, do or dare. What happens is one of the girls would spin the bottle and whoever it pointed to she'd give you a dare. You didn't do it you'd to skull a can but if you did, she had to give you a reward. So to cut a long story short, on the very first go, Lua Cavanagh spins the bottle and of course who does it land on but myself. Across the fire I seen her slant her eye, too, as much as to say maybe she done that on purpose. I've an idea she half liked me. She was always slagging me on account of my accent so she was, but in a kind of a flirty way that I did fucking love to hear her doing.

Now I forgot to say, along with the booze and the firelighters we'd stashed in the shed, there was a couple of spray-cans. If you want your reward, she goes, pouting her lips and blowing a few kisses, you've gotta write Lua Cavanagh Rocks! three times inside of the hanged man's house. That's what we called the gaff on the end, the hanged man's house. I looked at the others and then looked at the way she was looking at me through the fire, daring me on. Ok, says I, you're on. Then she shakes her braid and points one lovely finger up at the stars. Upstairs, she goes. Upstairs? Fuck sake! The problem there wasn't just that that was where they'd found the body dangling. The problem was there was no bleedin' stairs! There wasn't even much of a ceiling for Jaysus' sake! When they'd found McHugh there'd been a ladder he'd brung out with him but of course that was long since gone. My heart was pounding. Ok smart arse, says I, but how are you going to know if I done it or not? And then I seen, dangling out of the finger she's got pointing upwards, there's this little digital camera. Fair enough.   My heart is now literally banging against my throat so it is. And you're talking a real kiss, Lua, none of your messing with a peck on the cheek or any of that nonsense. Come back with the bleedin' proof young fella, she goes, ripping the shite out of my accent, and d'you see that bottle of Mickey Finn, reet? I'll let you drink dat out of me moute so I will. Jesus Christ when she said that about drinking the Mickey Finn out of her mouth, I was ready to write the Irish Proclamation on them four walls never mind Lua Cavanagh Rocks! I fairly grabbed the camera off of her and before I'd time to even think what I was going to do I'd grabbed up a spray-can and was standing in what would've been the hall of the show room, staring up at the constellations through the gaps in the rafters.

The other thing I forgot to mention was how we also kept a couple of torches in that shed. The one I had with me was small enough you could just about hold it in your teeth, so climbing up onto the second floor wasn't going to be too much of a major difficulty. I was always good at climbing. The only problem was now, standing on my Toblers looking up at the rafters, I was starting to feel just a little bit less enthusiastic. To make matters a whole lot worse, I was after hearing up above what might've been rats or what might've been one of the lads messing if it wasn't for the fact that I'd left them all lying round the campfire half twisted.

Ah fuck it says I you're imagining things, just get it over with, and I began to shimmy and haul myself up through a kind of a missing trapdoor and onto the rafters where the ceiling would've gone eventually. I'd snagged my jeans on the way up and tore a hole in my shin but that was ok, they were old jeans and the way my heart was going I barely felt the scrape. So I'm lying sort of flat on my belly and one hand is already shaking the can, and so then I pull the torch out of my mouth and I'm about to have a look to see where I'm going to spray her beautiful name and then I swear to God the heart literally leapt out of me.

How I didn't fall back through that missing trapdoor I do not know. I can still see it to this day, caught up in the circle of torchlight. Over by the wall, a face that white it was like chalk so it was. I dropped the torch but it must've been on a string coz it didn't fall through the gaps and when I recovered my nerve and shone it up again I knew it was himself and he was huddled up in the corner in the very spot his dad was found hanging, and he panting like a rabbit that's cornered. So I start saying his name, over and over, and showing him I don't mean him any harm.

Once I had him calmed down I could see he was in a bad way. Later on the doc said he was suffering from dehydration and exposure. And shock. Shock! Jaysus he wasn't the only one! I'd nothing I could give him to drink but he was shivering, so I wrapped my hoody around him, and then I shouted and whistled and hollered for an absolute age because besides being half pissed the lads must've thought I was messing with them. But after about a fucking half-hour, eventually two of them appears underneath in the hallway below and Lua standing behind them, with her mouth and eyes open like she's watching a high-wire act. And sure maybe that's what it was.

So to cut a long story short, after I'd lowered himself through to the two lads, coming down out of that trap I fell awkward and fractured my ankle. With the result that I spent the next six weeks on crutches. And that wasn't so bad, but of course the Ma bet fair hell out of me, didn't I tell you not to go in there messing around the estates you fucking eejit.

And I never did get the wear out of Lua Cavanagh. Though I do dream an odd time I'm tasting Mickey Finn out of her perfect mouth. But you know what? I think I might've gone up in her estimation. So you never know. We live and hope. As the Da would say.

Recissa Vegetior Assurgit

So ran the college motto. It was cast in wrought-iron lettering beneath the crest atop the gates. It was legible in the mosaic underfoot as one stepped through the doors. It was at the masthead of the occasional college correspondence. Few other students seemed aware of it. But to Patch Kearney, its Latin had the grandeur of an incantation: a promise; a menace. *Recissa Vegetior Assurgit*. Cut back, it revives 'more lustily. A gardening metaphor, he supposed. The old seminary could trace its resurgence to the late eighteenth century, to Grattan's Parliament and the easing of the penal laws. In those days, the church had been brutally hacked. Then it resurged, with all the glamour of the repressed.

Patch looked at the magnificent old magnolia the thin March sun had once again tricked into life, its branches bowed like candelabra under wax flames. In the circles of clay beneath the trees of the college grounds, paper daffodils and tiny blue and white flowers whose names escaped him flickered anomalously in the cold breeze. Jug, jug, jug went the machinery, driving piles into the regurgitated earth where the new Arts Centre was to be built.

Recissa Vegetior Assurgit. It was a trick that Nature was consummately good at pulling off. Towns and cities, too. But Patch was fifty-seven, and he felt every year of it. The cobwebs of another hangover didn't help. It was Saturday, and the seminary turned college had an abandoned look, its rows of windows lifeless and unseeing. There was only one car parked on the semi-circle of gravel reserved for the staff, a purple Volkswagen Passat, *Baby On Board*. Was he late? Patch checked his watch. He was early. Time for a last cigarette.

— There's very little I can do for you. You know the rules, Patrick. One percent for every day late, simple as. The rules have to be the same for everyone.
— I understand. I wasn't looking to be treated any differently…
What should he call her… Dr Neale? Patricia? He grimaced. *Miss*?
— For an essay extension I'd need a medical cert. You know the procedure.

— It's not an extension I'm after either…

— What, then?

— I wanted…I don't know. He looked around the office, as though the answer might be there. Bookshelves and papers, in academic disregard for order. A family photo. A pot plant.

— I wanted to apologise. I think.

— To *aplogise*? Patrick, there's no need…

— No. Let me… Please. When I was being interviewed…do you remember? You were on the committee that interviewed me.

Trish Neale shrugged. If she remembered the interview, which she supposed she vaguely did, she wasn't at all sure what bearing it could have on the present case. Patch Kearney had been in college for the better part of two years now. A harmless character, by all accounts. But hopelessly unreliable.

— At the interview there was you, there was Dr Kinsella, and the old chaplain was there. I forget his name.

— Fr John.

— Fr John! It was early June. I think. I do remember I was in mortal terror. My hands get the shakes. When I'm nervous, I mean, not... The three of you were lined up like the three inquisitors. See no evil, speak no evil. Ha ha! I was ready to… I wanted to be anywhere but here. I wanted to tell you all how sorry I was for wasting your time. Then to make a bolt for it! But then, before we even began, you told me the interview was no more than a formality.

He glanced up at Trish Neale. Her eyes were on him, brown, mildly bemused, her eyebrows hoisted into an attitude of: *'where is any of this going?'* He looked down at his fingers, nail-bitten, nicotine-stained. Where was any of this going?

— It was very kind of you. To say that.

He took a deep breath. Over the years, you get out of the habit of talking to people.

— All part of the job, Mr Kearney.

Not meeting her eyes, he drew another deep breath.

— I didn't want to say it at the time, at the interview I mean, but…

But. During his first year in college, Patricia Neale had been away on maternity leave. There were other lecturers he felt he knew better. Or that knew him better: his eccentricities; his *issues*. But she was second-year academic adviser, so that was that.

Besides, she had an approachable face. Shrewd, vaguely ironic, at times just a shade world-weary. Her baby had been born with a hole in its heart. He knew this because at start of term they'd remembered it (him? her?) in their prayers at the oratory. It was on account of this complication that she was here, today, while her baby was up in St Dymphna's for observation.

So she'd been away all the time the old duffer had tried to adjust to the human zoo of third level education. And then, too, she was from Dublin. A blow-in. Poor ould Patch, they called him about the town ever since he'd returned from London after his lost decades. Poor ould Patch, sure he's a *craytur*! Only when the whiskey got the better of him, then he wasn't such a craytur...

He noticed there was a crucifix on the wall. Was she a believer? Certainly, he'd seen the smudge of ash on her forehead the Wednesday before last. But what did that say? It was a rare member of staff who didn't don that badge for the day that was in it. And as for crucifixes, there was no shortage of them about the halls and corridors. Relics from a different geological era, just as on Discovery Channel you get marine fossils high on a mountain.

Was she a believer? He wanted her to be one. The new breed of professional, confident and atheistic, dismayed him. All his life Patch had struggled with his faith. God knows there'd been times he'd strayed far. Two years up in Maynooth had been enough to cure him of any thoughts of a vocation. He'd had his fair share of disappointments. But then, too, he'd disappointed. And in London, when he'd hit the bottle, there'd been no stopping him.

When news finally reached him that his father was dead, he'd returned. The town had moved on far more than he had. He was fifty-four. His life stretched as empty as a tundra. He was hounded by loneliness. One day, as he shambled along the river with the old dog, a few shafts of sunlight through the black cloud had picked out the spire of the cathedral. The octagonal tower was modelled, they said, on a guildhall in Bruges. He knew the seminary next door to the cathedral was a college these days. He understood what was being asked of him. Two weeks later, his heart skipping like a bird in a cage, he'd filled out an application in the public library. That same night he'd slipped it into the college letterbox.

That first year had been a continual struggle. Not so much with the material, though writing essays had frustrated him. When he'd read Chaucer or Plato, back in his bed-sit or on a park bench, it was like stained-glass illuminating the dismal interior of his week. No. It was people he'd had to adjust to. The brashness of youth. Being around them. Being amongst them. Being ignored by them. It's true there was a smattering of mature students. Five or six of them would congregate around the same table in the canteen, presided over by a big-busted divorcee with an eye for the younger men. By and large he'd kept his distance. There was one student only he got on with. A smoker, like himself. An African girl. Nigerian, was it? He'd often bump into her on the fag-strewn gravel by the back door. After several weeks, they'd fallen into conversation. Like himself, Charity was a loner. Charity, who covered her teeth with her hand whenever she laughed.

His mind had been wandering, all the time that he'd been speaking. Now he became aware that he'd stopped speaking. The office had filled with silence. Dr Neale was looking at him, and she was no longer bemused.

— So you're... *barred?*

— I guess so.

— Patch. Why do you drink whiskey? I mean I can understand anyone drinking once in a while. Sort of. You know you're not supposed to, but... I mean, we're none of us angels.

Her eyes had drifted onto the family photo. Patch glanced away, having no wish to violate her privacy.

— Everyone needs a blow-out, once in a while. But what I don't understand is, why *whiskey?* When you tell me you know what it does to you...

He looked again at his hands. The skin on his right knuckles was ragged. Why whiskey? Why *whiskey?* As far as he knew it was the same damn chemical as any other spirit! But once he'd fix on the amber bottle behind the bar, once he'd smell or taste it, he'd know he was straight back on the slope.

— And it was you who started it?

— D'you know, I honestly can't remember. The whiskey... does that.

— Don't blame the whiskey, Patch.

But he wasn't. He'd simply meant that when he'd hurtle down that slope, the following morning would have wiped all specifics

77

from his memory. There'd be a metal taste in his mouth, and an unspecified guilt as flighty as paranoia that mightn't leave him for days on end. But few if any images to account for it.

He gave her a watery smile. Why whiskey, when he knew it made him an ugly drunk, and is there anything worse than that? He looked again at the pink scabs across his knuckles.

— I remember I fetched him one good belt in the gob, and he went down what's more! I think maybe I'd seen him acting the maggot with some of the first years.

— But you can't be sure.

No, he couldn't be sure. He could be sure of very little, once he'd smelt the sweet, cut-grass aroma rising from the glass.

Patricia Neale fought down the urge to guffaw, not least because the story had taken her completely by surprise. It seemed incongruous that this individual sitting before her — hadn't he at one time trained for the priesthood or something? — should've turned brawler! Sixty, if he was a day, and always so soft-spoken. Life in the old dog yet, she all but smirked. And that other blackguard had a name that stank to high heaven about the town. He'd been asking for a good hiding for months. But a scrap in a pub was scarcely something she could be expected to condone. She composed a frown.

— We might have to report this, Patrick.

— I understand that.

To keep the smirk under wraps, she shook her head and consulted her watch.

— I'll have to think about it. Are you in on Monday?

— I can be.

— Ok let me think it over. I'll talk to you Monday.

The interview was over. He stood, and was again awkward.

— How's...ahm?

He mimed rocking a baby.

— Oh, she's great. They're delighted with her. I'm just running up to Dymphna's this minute to pick her up.

He smiled and looked down. As he stepped into the corridor her voice overtook him.

— Patch?

— ...?

— Don't tell anyone else about the fight. Huh?

He stood by the great magnolia, its limbs swaying in the breeze. Beneath it, a smattering of starlings were stabbing the earth and flipping the black leaves. They were aggressive birds, sharp enough to sit out the winter without emigrating. Soon, presumably, they'd be nesting.

Jug, jug, jug went the pile-driving machinery.

The semi-circle of gravel before the college was empty now. The purple Passat had gone to collect the *Baby on Board*. The child with the hole in her heart would be seeing her first spring after all; he, his fifty-seventh. His eyes wandered up to the dark window of Dr Neale's office. That scuffle hadn't been what he'd wanted to say to her. That hadn't been what he'd come in here for. But you get out of the habit of talking.

With Charity Alfa, the Nigerian girl, he'd go for coffee once or twice a week. They shared an elective in psychology on Tuesdays and an ethics tutorial on Thursday mornings. They'd go for lunch, maybe. Even, once, for afternoon drinks. She never went out in the evenings, she told him. Far too much work to be getting on with! He'd said none of this to Trish Neale.

Why whiskey? she'd asked him. Why *whiskey*? He could've told her that one. Maybe he should've told her. He hadn't once touched whiskey, not since induction day at the college eighteen months ago. There'd been late essays; there'd been lost weekends. You can't teach an old dog new tricks! But he'd given whiskey a wide berth.

He shook his head.

That evening… *That* evening (was it two days ago? three?), as he was shambling towards his bed-sit, there were voices coming from under the bridge. Young voices. Then all at once a laugh had rung out. It echoed from the shadowy wall to the far side of the river. It was a throaty laugh; an African laugh. It was her laugh.

The blow to his solar plexus took him entirely by surprise. He'd leaned weakly at the parapet of the bridge. For a while he'd watched the shadows, playing grotesquely over the far wall. He heard again the unbridled laugh resonate from under the arch of the bridge.

Five minutes later, Patch stopped into Racy Byrne's. His eyes had run through the rainbow of colours behind the bar. But as yet he pointed to a clear spirit. Where the hell was this tumour inside him after coming from? Where, this hollow? The girl was half his age. If even! She laughed freely, and at the same time she covered her teeth with her hand. He'd never once thought of her 'that way'. True, she'd told him she'd be working on an ethics assignment all that night. So she'd lied. What about it? He thought of the shadows stretching like a Chinese lantern show. He thought of the laugh, throaty and youthful. He was fifty-seven, for the love of God! Well out of all that... And now, this voracious ache had ambushed him. Was there a word for it? Jealousy didn't fit the bill. Whatever it was, it had him miserable.

Why whiskey? she'd asked.

Why the hell not?

The starlings cavorted away, raucous and aggressive. Passing through the gates, Patch shook his head up at the college motto. What the hell are you supposed to do with an emotion like that, once it resurges?

The White Van

Fewer people were taking the air now. It was that in-between time, when the sea is more luminous than the sky, as though it retains the memory of the day. All the length of the promenade, neon streetlights had begun to flicker on. A spasm gripped Claire, and she flicked up her collar. The breeze off the skittish waves was stiffening, and to her back the harbour was coming alive with a frenetic tinkering of stays against masts.

The turmoil inside her was no less frantic. It clamoured at her throat, causing it to constrict. It caught at her breathing. When she tried to concentrate, it caused waves of loose emotion to toss her thoughts about like so much flotsam. Where was the mistake made? *When* was the mistake made? She couldn't fix on anything long enough to turn it into a solid, dependable fact. Everything followed the absurd logic of a bad dream. Only the giddy anxiety had any reality.

That morning she had been calm. Wonderfully so. It was her day with the children.

She'd picked up Liam about two, and from the window Sam had watched her strap him into the baby seat. He'd even waved, briefly. She remembered that. Traffic was heavy, though, and she'd been late getting to the school.

Most of the kids were already gone. But she could make out an anorak and ponytail hovering by the entrance. She knew it was Sorcha from the red schoolbag. One of the teachers, she wasn't sure which, was waiting with her. Just as her car pulled in, though, the teacher put a hand on Sorcha's ponytail and ushered her inside. Claire immediately swung the door open. Before she hopped out, she glanced into the mirror, *Mammy'll be back in two ticks honey, all right?* Liam's mouth opened *fa fa fa*. She held up two fingers, as though her lamb could count. *Two ticks.*

The teacher must have taken Sorcha into the Principal's Office because the corridor was empty, with that intense vacancy peculiar to public buildings. *Yoo-hoo! Sorcha!* There was no answer. She glanced back at her car. Had she locked it? She was on the point of returning to check when a voice overtook her. *Mrs Delaney?* It was Mr Peters, the deputy principal. From behind his leg Sorcha was showing off the gap in her teeth. *I, ahm*, Claire gestured vaguely, as though she were being accused of something. She often felt she was being accused of something. *Traffic…*

Ach sure she's no trouble at all, are you Sorcha-Dorcha? Sorcha clung to the mighty thigh and giggled.

The whole thing can't have taken more than two minutes. She nodded thanks and hurried Sorcha as far as the car and had just depressed the button on the key-ring when her heart stopped dead. The baby-seat was empty. The strap, unbuckled. She pulled open the rear door. Nothing.

Liam! she called. *Li-am!*

Mammy where's Liam? frowned Sorcha.

There was a white van parked directly opposite. A red-faced man on a mobile phone was in the driver's seat. Claire lifted Sorcha into the back seat, *just stay there honey*. She shut the door, locked it, hurried across the road. Still in conversation, the man shrugged at her frightened gesture. She rat-tatted at the window with her key. The man frowned, but he opened the window. *Sorry I'm parked over there*, she glanced about, horrified that the car was again alone. She swallowed, breathed. *You didn't see anyone…near the car? What love? While I was gone. I was just picking up…look, there wasn't anyone near the car was there?* The man blew out and glanced at his phone. Perhaps the call was important. *Not while I was sat here anyways love.* But she was already running back across the road. She paused at the car, patted the roof to reassure Sorcha, and hurried into the corridor *Mr Peters! Mr Peters!* As they hastened back outside she explained. His frown terrified her.

Liam! he roared. *Liam!* she whimpered.

That was when she saw the white van pulling away.

Oh Christ! She should've stopped it! She had to… *He's in…he's in the…*

She turned to Peters. He was staring at her, *Are you…?*

The van, she panted.

Have you an inhaler? She shook her head. *Pills? Medication?* She shut her eyes and again she saw the van pull away. She stumbled as far as her car. Her phone was in the glove compartment. She had to call Sam. Mr Peters was following… *No! The van! Stop the…*

She had to follow the van. It was stopped at the lights. She mustn't let it get away. She fumbled at the door. The traffic-lights were already changing. At last it opened. And there, there, nestling between the driver's pedals and looking up at her from behind her huge sunglasses, was Liam.

She thought Sam would see the funny side; the mad chase that had never happened. Can you imagine if Peters had caught up with the guy! Instead, deliberately mistaking her giggles, he was furious. *Christ is it any wonder!* He had pulled the bottle of pills out of her fist and was shaking them as though they were to blame, *How many of these did you take? But it wasn't my fault* she told him *I was gone for two minutes. Two.*

And what if he had been taken away in the van what then eh? Christ what was I thinking, letting you pick Sorcha up from school. Never again I can tell you that much.

The wind caught her, and sent shivers through her. The rind of a moon was following where the sun had long since sunk. *Clink clink* jangled the boats.

Oh God don't let me fall back into depression.

The sea was dark now. It would be so cold as to hurt like a toothache. But that wasn't something she could do. That wasn't something she would ever do.

It wasn't my fault, she told the black waves. *It wasn't my fault. It wasn't.*

The Lodger

The third argument decided the matter. Abruptly, during the wash-up, he threw in the towel. Ok ok, we'll take a lodger, Jesus!

She didn't rise to the bait. Sufficient unto the day was the victory thereof. Who was it, she might well have asked, who told her whenever he lost his job that they'd have to find a way to bring in a few pounds? As if she didn't realise that well enough herself without him spelling it out for her. But he was the man, so where was the point of arguing. I'll put a wee announcement up on the notice-board she whispered on the morning following, just as she was setting out for work. You get a better class of people working in a hospital. He rolled over and grunted. I'll run on so or I'll be late.

Some hours after she had left, Maguire wandered into their daughter's room and sat on the bed. Chiara was studying Arts down in Dublin this last year. Trinity College, his old alma mater. He lifted the photo from the bedside table: there she was with a few bikini-clad girlfriends, squeezing grins together over rainbow coloured cocktails inside some trashy bar in Malaga. There'd been tears and tantrums in the run-up to that particular jaunt. Still, he'd supported her when she'd decided for Arts, and even helped find her lodgings through a few old acquaintances. How was she going to take it when she heard they were letting out her room? But hadn't that been the bones of his argument from the first. What'll Chiara say love? She'll have to like it or lump it, won't she? Who does she imagine is going to pay for her *Arts* degree I should like to know? The accent, so sharp it might have been stropped on the incessant westerlies that swept down from Divis. Ach, she was right, he supposed. The mortgage had to be paid. And that whipper-snapper in the bank wasn't about to restructure for a second time, not now his redundancy money was well and truly spent.

*

The first person to answer the ad was Nigerian. There was a baby, who stared out from a colourful sling over the woman's shoulder.

They smiled weakly, showed her around as if apologising for the place, and agreed the instant the front door was shut on her departure that the room was eminently unsuitable for a young mother.

Several days passed.

On the Sunday there was a telephone enquiry of kinds, a crank call perhaps. One way or another, the caller never showed on the next evening but one. When she came in from the night shift, he looked at her as much as to say well, where's all the prospective lodgers then? These things take time, she replied into the mirror, undressing as she always did these days with her back to him. It's worth waiting for the right *class* of person. And then, so as not to concede ground, hi, have you told Chiara yet? Why would we upset her, aren't we as well to wait until such time as we've actually *found* someone to take the room? I don't know, you mollycoddle that girl so you do. She's not a child anymore you know.

Not a *chayld* anymore. It was true, all the same. Hadn't Chiara informed them at Christmas she was putting in for a J1 visa; there were three of them supposed to head over to Boston for the summer. It was that that freed up the room in the first place. But she was only nineteen. The room had been her den, from the day they'd moved in. Her clothes were hanging in the wardrobe. That was her name on the door, her posters on the walls.

Several weeks went by. They talked of the plan less and less. But then, they talked less and less. Each seemed to be adopting a policy of wait and see.

A letter came from the bank. They were going to cut his overdraft facility from £2500 to £500, and requested a repayment plan on the balance. Another notified them the interest rate on their mortgage was going up by twenty-five basis points. Nothing for it, she told him. You'll just have to go in and have another wee word with that famous bank manager. Reluctantly, he made an appointment for the Friday. Then, on the Wednesday, she breezed in with an energy he hadn't seen about her in a long time. There'd been a text. Someone wanted to see the room so they did.

Who is it? I don't know, some fellow. Has a name, does he? He has a foreign name, just a second. Aye, Artürus. His name is Artürus. And he works at the hospital, this *Artürus*? I don't know,

I imagine he must. You *imagine*? Am I supposed to know every living soul that works in the hospital now? Wasn't that the whole point, his expression said, of putting up the ad on the staff noticeboard? They obeyed a truce while he served up the dinner. Afterwards, he let her do most of the straightening up. He won't come, he yawned, when at last he flicked over to the ten o'clock news. More grim figures from the Chancellor. There'd been a woman found strangled in a college dorm in Oxford. Some child or other had been abducted in broad daylight from Windsor Park. That was when the doorbell rang.

*

The caller was so pale as to look undernourished. There were deep thumbprints of insomnia pressed beneath each eye. His hair was lank, and although he was a couple of inches taller than either one of them, he somehow gave the impression of a smaller being. You must be Artūrus she all but laughed. Artūrus, yes. Come in come on, you must be frozen!

What do you do, Mr Artūrus, if you don't mind me asking you? She fired a warning look at him, don't you dare! I am student, said the other.

Maguire let her get on with showing the *student* around. Surely it was obvious even to her there was no great point giving the room to a *student*. Isn't that what Chiara was, down below? Besides there was something creepy about him: the lifeless hair; the pallor; the eyes that looked just below yours. Where did you say you're *from* Artūrus? she chimed as she led him back into the living-room. From Lithuania. How much is rent? This question was addressed in his direction, and he fired out the sum of £300 by reflex before his wife had a chance to speak. Her open beak and dagger-look left no doubt as to the extravagance of the amount. But the caller considered, nodded, pulled a fat wallet from inside his parka and counted out the sum in new twenties, all from the mainland too. And a month's deposit Maguire trumped, as though the gesture of meeting the sum had been in some way a reproach. The youth again appeared to consider, again nodded, and counted out another £300, laying the entire bundle meticulously on the table with long, thin fingers. Oh my, said his wife, still staring daggers

86

from behind the caller's shoulder, we never expected for a minute sir you'd be carrying so much about you in cash! Well, she flashed her death smile at her husband and, tapping the pile of twenties, that's settled then. When do you want to move in? Maybe tomorrow. Tomorrow, aye. Could you make it maybe Friday, would that be all right? It's just we've a few wee things to clear out of the room. To make it ready for you. Friday, yes, is ok Friday.

The youth didn't seem to want to move. The married couple exchanged glances. Do you have key? he asked the woman at length, blinking like an owl. Maguire looked from his wife to the ceiling and clicked his fingers energetically. Would you believe it, I never thought of having one copied! Her enormous smile did not reach as far as her eyes. Well, give him yours. He'll give you his, Artürus, that's my husband for you, he has a head like a sieve so he does. How can I copy it, dear, if I give mine to him? Well I'll give him mine then and let you copy yours tomorrow, just be sure you're not out whenever I get back home from the hospital.

Not *oyt*. Of an evening was he ever *oyt*?

That night they talked long into the small hours. I just don't like him; he gives me the creeps. Well it's past decided; you took the money quick enough. That's another thing, where's a *student* supposed to get that sort of money, there must have been over a thousand sterling in that wallet, and all Bank of England, did you mind that? Well what about it, I daresay he must've come over through Heathrow or something. When? When what? When did he come over through Heathrow? Well I don't know. Because it's April love, what sort of *student* course starts up in April? What are you trying to say exactly? Nothing, I just don't fancy the thought of him moping about the house all day is all. Well if he is, can't *you* keep an eye on him, you that's always *in*? And what's that supposed to mean? Nothing. Nothing? I just think you're being stupid about it is all. Stupid, right. She sensed she had gone too far, and nuzzled up to him. It'll give you something to say to that wee whipper-snapper in the bank. He blew out, I suppose. You'll have to clear up her things into the attic. I left a few boxes under the stairs. Right. And you won't forget to get a key cut now sure you won't? Hardly. Oh go on with you! she said, poking him lightly. Hi and you better call up Chiara, tell her the room's let out.

He rolled over. She'd had her way, as per usual.

What hurt Maguire most was the breezy matter-of-factness with which Chiara received the news. He'd spent a long, painful morning packing her most intimate things into cardboard boxes. If he'd been still working he'd never have let himself get so sentimental about it. But this weather his emotions seemed to be at the whim of every petty setback, worry, memory, concern, hope, row and disappointment. What would the men he'd worked with think if they could see the state of him now? This time two years back by God that banker's snide smile would've scarcely raised more than a disdainful laugh from him; nowadays it had him on tenterhooks. Ever since those bloody circulars, he'd been rehearsing and rehearsing what he might say or should say but probably wouldn't have the calmness or presence of mind to say in that poky little office on Friday.

His hands were shaking, too, as they carefully folded away his daughter's clothes. Even after the books and make-up had been boxed, the room was still Chiara's; it was *her* duvet, *her* desk, *her* curtains over the tiny window. Everything spoke of her, even down to the luminous stars he'd helped her place about the ceiling all those years ago. And now the sanctity of her room was to be given over to that whey-face? He'd been putting the dreaded phone call on the long finger all day, and when finally she answered her mobile (there was the sound of people chatting in the background) his *what your mother and I have decided* came out in a phlegmy voice he scarcely recognised as his own. Course you have to Daddy, sure I'll be away in Boston!

The trip to the bank, over which his gut turned many a somersault, was brief and peremptory. Nothing whatsoever could be done about the hike of twenty-five base points we understand your distress Mr Maguire but you have to understand that the standard variable rates are set with reference to the blah blah blah blah beyond our control yes of course that's good news that you'll have *some* rental income coming in Mr Maguire but when it comes to your overdraft facility the limit depends you see on the amount of money going through your account on a *regular* basis and our records show that for eighteen months now blah blah blah blah. Mr Maguire? What? So that's the best we can do I'm afraid.

A double espresso in a nearby greasy spoon did nothing to calm his agitation. Quite the opposite. The bank that likes to say yes! Six-seven years ago they couldn't press enough money onto him. Yes sir no sir three bags full sir. But now that a man was down on his luck? His soul was in such a state of turmoil as he entered the house that he'd forgotten they now had a lodger. He was jolted by the apparition of a pallid figure loitering about the kettle. The curt nod of the lank hair may not have been surly, but Maguire's embarrassment at the start he'd just received made him hypersensitive. He looked from the wan, ironic smile and lowered eyes to the mug that stood on the counter beneath them: it was Chiara's. You like coffee Mr? No, and please be good enough not to use our daughter's mug.

A month went by.

I tell you he gives me the heebie-jeebies. If he's supposed to be studying, why is he forever hanging about the place? Well it might be an online course, there's plenty of those in this day and age. I know all about online courses. You needn't tell me about online courses. But answer me this, if that's what it's supposed to be, could he not just as well do it from Transylvania or wherever the hell he comes from? You're being *styup*-id again. Am I? Then tell me, why did he want a key for Chiara's room, sure that room was never locked. Well, what about it, wouldn't you want your privacy? Privacy is it? Tell me another thing have you ever passed by that door at two or three in the morning? Why, what about it? There's a queer blue light you can make out underneath the door. Well? I'm telling you it's not normal, that damned clickedy-clackedy going on all hours of the night, he must never sleep, our friend. You've a right to let *me* sleep, she yawned, I'm away out at six so I am. Ok, just you put your ear to the door at six, you'll hear him right enough. Tsst! What does he be doing in there anyway? Maguire asked, but she'd already begun to snore.

*

One morning − she wasn't on the roster that week − the lodger said maybe you like try Lithuanian food Mrs Magweer? Ach, for God's sake will you call me Sinead! If you like I cook some kugela, is traditional dish. Did you hear that Henry? Artūrus says he's going to cook us a traditional Lithuanian dish! Maguire, who was out the back, let on not to hear. A week before, the interloper had brought back a bunch of bruised yellow roses, God only knows where he'd got them, and he did not care one bit for the way his missus had clucked ach isn't that very thoughtful they're lovely so they are while she snipped the stems herself but had him dust off the old vase that for years had stood idle as a reproach atop the cupboard. He thought twice, and stuck his head in through the window, there's those gigot chops I want to use up love. Her eyes narrowed. Tell you what we'll do Artūrus, can you hold off cooking up your meal till Friday, would that be all right, only Chiara'll be up home then you see, that's our daughter, it'll be a nice surprise for her, something so *exotic*.

Maguire marched back into the tool shed, but his hands were shaking so much they refused to handle the drill. If she'd wanted to wound him, she could've picked no better weapon. When first he was laid off, Maguire had thrown himself into all sorts of home improvement projects, and had pursued every blessed job opening for which he was even halfway qualified. But as the months went by and his energy was sapped by the silence and dull routines, the kitchen had become his domain. He was inventive even on the tightest budget, and could for a while lose himself in chopping vegetables the way he once used to lose himself over a lathe. It was the one area she still allowed him take pride in. Well she knew that with Chiara home on a flying visit to make final preparations for her long summer abroad, he would have pulled out all the stops. There was even a plump leg of lamb he'd eyed up in Hamiltons; but there'd been no way he could've asked for that on tick anymore. He threw down the drill and sat on his hands, to stop their shaking.

*

How d'you like the wee room? Chiara was sitting up on the counter, nibbling at the corner of her thumb. The whole house smelt of roasting garlic. Is nice, the stars. Oh God, are they still there? His hands cuffed in Maguire's oven gloves, Artūrus shrugged yes. I asked your father to take them down, put in Sinead Maguire who was lighting candles on the festive table, her hair put up elegantly, but sure you know what he's like for getting anything done! From the hallway Maguire heard them. He'd been

90

making quite a thing of pulling out all the boxes filled with her things from the attic and dusting off the two old suitcases. Earlier he'd said to Chiara he'd head on down to Dublin on the train with her Sunday to see her off. Ach no need Daddy sure I've a lift with one of the girls so I have! With all the bustle and activity in the kitchen, he'd scarcely had a solitary moment to have a word with her, his only child that he hadn't seen since Christmas.

He was silent during the meal, a baked affair that was glorified potato and diced bacon so far as he could see. He wasn't lying when he said that his tummy was feeling a bit dodge, though from the expression on his wife's face he might just as well have been. But wasn't that a woman all over? In fact, there'd been a tightness in his gut all day. He could have really done with that trip down to Dublin, to get a breath of air away from the cramped estates with their ridiculous bunting. Of course, *she* wasn't long getting her revenge. Leave those, his wife said as Artürus was gathering up the dishes for the sink, that's old sour-puss's job! And it was all he could do not to clatter and bang as the three of them sat around the living-room in the candlelight, sipping their Baileys.

*

Most mornings, at eight-forty, Artürus was in the habit of taking a shower. Usually he locked the bedroom door behind him. Maguire knew this because anytime he happened to pass and heard the shower running, he tried it. This he did more by force of habit than with anything particular in mind. If the door were suddenly to open, chances are he'd just peep inside the briefest moment before moving on to the kitchen.

This conjecture was put to the test about two weeks after Chiara had set off, tearfully in the end, for the States. One morning the door gave. He at once closed it back over, then stared hard at the bathroom door as if trying to see through it. There was a steady shush from within, and overhead a reassuring gurgle from the attic pipes. Maguire's heart was pounding. In an instant, he was inside the room. At once he was physically struck by the acrid stench of the confined young male, a stale mixture of sweat, sprays and effluvia that set him on edge. The light was off and the curtains tightly drawn, but by the eerie blue effulgence of

91

the two humming computer screens he could see there were clothes strewn about the floor, and that the duvet was thrown back. Unable to help himself he edged into the interior.

Maguire was no great shakes at computers, though he had signed up for a basic IT course (she'd pushed him to 'upskill') in the early days of his unemployment. It was sufficient for him to recognise that the tiny hourglasses and infinitesimally advancing lines meant that unto each laptop something weighty was being downloaded. He turned from the blinking screens to the bed. Was it a trick of the submarine light, or were there lemon-coloured stains extending variously over the undersheet? He had no time to check. From outside he heard the crunch of a lock turning. Overhead the pipes were gurgling, but the hiss of the shower had stopped.

Maguire leapt to the door and twisted outside, and had only just time to pull the door shut behind him before the lodger's white back flecked with pimples edged out from the bathroom. He was clad only in a towel, and clutched in his hand an open toilet bag. I was just ahm, said Maguire, indicating with his thumb the way to the kitchen, I was about to stick on the kettle. Artürus looked at him without answering, for once meeting his eye squarely. In all the months he'd been there, he'd barely had a civil word from this man. He shook his wet hair as though he had seen right through Maguire's purpose, edged past him into the room, pressed the door shut and turned the key in the lock.

Maguire was never sure after that whether Artürus had seen his hand fly from the door handle and into his dressing-gown pocket. What he was increasingly sure of was the sardonic edge to the silent smirk which the interloper had directed towards him from the very first. He wasn't entirely blameless of course, he hadn't exactly welcomed him in with open arms the way his wife had. But there was something preternatural about this surly youth, and in spite of the mounting arrears and the final warning letter from the bank he hadn't as yet shown to herself, Maguire would be only too glad to see the back of him. In fact he was holding news of that letter from her until the issue of expelling this intruder was resolved. The sight of the besmirched sheet stretched over Chiara's innocent bed had removed any last shred of doubt or conscience.

Tell us love do you do his laundry? I do not, whatever put that into your head? Because he's an unhygienic young fella I can tell you that much. He's no such thing, now I don't know what it is between you and him, you're like two dogs circling so you are. And that's my fault is it? I don't know what your problem is but you've never once made the lad feel welcome that much I do know. Do you know what he does be doing in that room at all hours? What 'does he be doing'? *Downloading*. Probably all kinds of porn. Ach will you give over your nonsense, porn! And he has the place a pigsty. She froze and stared at him. Did you go into his room? Henry Maguire did you go into his *room*?

Then she found the letter. What's this? Now, Maguire was certain that it wasn't he who'd left it lying out in the open. He'd placed it very carefully inside one of the cookbooks. Is this what I think it is? she screamed. This is dated last Monday *week* so it is! She slapped it down on the counter, flashed her eyes at him, and marched magnificently out of the kitchen. An hour later he heard the hall door slam behind her. Then it opened again briefly. Do not think you have heard the last of this mister! He heard the angry heels slap down the street. She was out for the night at a work do.

Maguire sat for a long time in the dark. At about ten o'clock the front door opened and Artürus slinked in. A carrier bag in which something clinked dangled from his arm. He hesitated, seeing the room in darkness, sensing Maguire's presence. He looked quickly from the armchair to the counter on which the envelope still lay. Then with a smirk he sidled along the wall and disappeared down the hallway that led to Chiara's room.

Two further things happened that night. Just before half past two a text arrived from his wife: *staying over with chand*. Chandani, he smiled wryly, or maybe one of the interns she was forever flirting with on the phone. It scarcely raised a jealous qualm in him now. Then, some time after three, the mobile burst into life. Daddy, a voice sobbed. Chiara? Honey? Daddy it's awful. The connection stuttered and cackled, but between her sobs and the many hiatuses he knew that his daughter was in distress, that a stalker had been hounding her, that she wanted to come home. The connection broke. There was no number in the call register by which he could dial back.

She wanted to come home. He all but wept to think of it. Because *how*? To *what* home? How much longer would it be a home? A reptile was ensconced there, defiling her bed, right now, this very hour. And even if there was a way to expel it and to cleanse the place, how could he protect her from the stalkers and predators of this filthy world? If he *could* make their house a haven, how long would it hold out before the bank reclaimed it?

Maguire rose, and opened the back door. A misshapen moon rising over the horizon had flattened the world to silhouettes, but it gave light enough to steer by. He made his way to the tool shed and opened the door quietly. For the first time in a long time his hand was steady. He knew what he had to do.

Maguire hesitated for a long time outside the room that had once been his daughter's. This night, there was no blue glow emanating from beneath the door, no flippant chattering of a keyboard. He rested his forehead against the wall and closed his eyes, as if praying. Then he looked up, patted his breast pocket, flicked open the lid of the jerrycan and began to splash paraffin over the hallway's carpet and wallpaper. As he did so he was aware that he, also, was being liberally splashed. And that was ok.

Rape

The clatter of unschooled metronomes told that the harbour was hard by. Within the visor of the rear-view mirror, Victor's eyes sought out mine. I could sense his smirk. Because it was an unmistakable music: the cantankerous dissonance of stay and shroud slapping each unsynchronised mast; the wind's unremitting tinkering with vane and windlass.

The bank-holiday seafront was tight with glimmering chrome. On our third pass, we slipped into a slot suddenly vacated. The three men swapped sudden jollities, swapped strident laughter. I pulled the door open, eager only to be in the air.

But I was in no humour for crowds.

I turned my back on the push-chairs; on the motorbikes eructating outside a beer-garden; on the tattooed man dragging his brat by the arm and giving leash to an erect bulldog; on the old woman's tongue moulding an ice-cream with the pressure of a cow moulding her calf. It was not yet eleven, and the sea air was already beginning to cloy with the sweet languor of candyfloss and frying onions.

Victor owned the boat. I didn't know his surname. I'd met him briefly the previous autumn on a refresher course down in Baltimore. It had ended, as such sessions do, with a vague exchange of numbers and good intentions. Now he was looking for crew. In truth, not one of us knew each other, not in any meaningful sense. That was why the men's laughs had so eager an edge. That's why my hand had stayed aware of the door handle.

As the others pulled on their oils beside his BMW, I watched the rhythmic slop of waves lifting the lazy harbour detritus. Within the walls, the water was tannin-stained, soiled by a tepid river dribbling relentless run-off from the bogs. But beyond the harbour-mouth the sea was champagne. I longed to be out there. I longed to be out there and alone.

'You sure you don't want to try these, love?' A hand, Thomas's, held out towards me a set of yellow waterproofs several sizes too large.

'I'll be fine.' My words sounded tart, so I looked at Victor and added, 'There's not a solitary cloud.'

'You'd be surprised. Once you're out there....' But he didn't press the point. It was evidently too early to risk the chauvinistic note.

To get to the boat, the *Nightingale*, we had to clamber over the decks of two trawlers slowly masticating a threesome of groaning tyres between their flanks. The tide must have been a good many hours from the full because the deck of the nearer, larger hulk was sunk some five or six feet below the pier. Its chamber below-decks boomed cavernously as each of the men dropped onto the metallic surface. Andrew, the tallest, offered me a tentative forearm. I laid a tentative hand on it, unsure what purpose it was supposed to serve, not wishing to give a wrong impression.

'Have you sailed much?'

'Not much.' Once more, it sounded curt, a retort. Now that I was on deck, my forehead was at a level with his chin. 'I did a course the summer before college.'

'Mirrors?'

'Lasers.'

'Very good.' His blue gaze was moving far above my hair to the opulent masts wagging and swaggering about the marina. Why wasn't Victor's *Nightingale* moored among them? He was a tax consultant, so far as I could remember, and must be worth a few bob. 'Nothing wrong with that,' Andrew smiled, his eyes still moving through the forest of dancing masts. It took me a moment to realise the remark related to my inexperience and not the dubious mooring.

We followed the others onto the second, lower trawler. The tough skin of the first was scabbed with rust and paint flakes, but it had the solidity of a permanent fixture. The deck of the smaller boat was livelier, and my body instinctively lowered its centre of gravity. I glanced about the precarious stacks of crates and salt-hoared lobster pots for anything I could grab onto if the need arose, careful to disguise my precautions from the men, careful to disguise how I was on the point of gagging at the cunt stench that emanated from the hold. I tried not to breathe until I'd crossed onto the yacht.

In the slick distending about the hull there floated the obscene nudity of a fish's belly. For some reason the gulls wouldn't touch

96

it. Their psychotic bickering sounded like derision. Turning away, I all but retched.

Gillian had warned me I was mad to be doing this.

'It's far too early girl.'

I'd looked into her aggravated eyes, and wondered whether it was concern or vicarious anger that was animating her.

'It's been three months,' I said, lighting up.

'But it's not as if you'll know any of them! Think about it Ellie…'

I took a long drag on the cigarette and looked hard at her. Then I blew the smoke into the night. 'That's just exactly the point.'

She shook her head. She wasn't prepared to let it go. To let me go. I began to feel resentful. 'Do you want me to end up like Hannah Phelan? Is that what you want?' She shook her head vaguely, as if she didn't know the story. Right! 'A month after it happened to Hannah, she dropped out of the Academy altogether. For God's sake she couldn't even be on her own in the same room with Mr Walsh!' She shook her head, as if she didn't know the man. 'The piano instructor?' I was suddenly furious. 'He's nearly seventy, Gill!'

Now her gaze was all concern, all wounded concern. 'That's not what I want. You know that's not what I want.'

I stubbed out the cigarette half-smoked, collapsing it on itself. Ach, it wasn't even her I was mad at. 'Just leave it, ok?'

'But you're crazy Ellie, do you know that? You told me yourself you won't know a single one of them. For all you know, there could be a…' She balked. I stared hard at her, daring her to finish. Her eyes deflected.

'You were saying?'

'You don't know the first thing about them, that's all.'

I dug my fingernails into my palm to calm the trembling. She noticed. So I unfurled my hand and began to revolve the ashtray on the table, and I spoke slowly and evenly. 'But that's how crewing works Gillian. I didn't know anyone in the string quartet when we toured last summer either.'

'The quartet!' She didn't say it. She didn't have to.

'From what this Victor guy said, I doubt they'll know each other, either. So we're all in the same boat.' How witty I was. She touched my hand and I withdrew it.

'Think girl.'

'Think what?'

'Think how's it going to feel when the boat moves off, and there's nowhere you can escape to.'

Think, girl. The two words slapped into my gut as Andrew's gentleman's arm now ushered me onto the squeaky white decking of the yacht. After the trawlers, it seemed confined, the scale model of a boat. Tommy was being clumsy about one of the cleats where a tie had got tangled. To get past I had to lay my hands on his shoulders. At first contact my palms shrank back, as though his oils carried a repulsive charge. So I pushed down on them, deliberately, and pivoted past him. Think, girl.

'What's the plan of action skipper?' This was Andrew. Victor was busy with charts and dividers. Behind his prematurely grey head I could see a receiver and a dead frequency dial. The key ring winked from the ignition. I realised my gut was taut, that I was anxious for the moment he would turn the key and a high whine would bring the displays to life.

'Nothing,' he replied without looking up. He was humming, happy with himself. Men are always happy when they're about some calculation. The dividers waddled stiff-kneed and comic across the chart, and it struck me that the deference we were showing him was unearned. On the Baltimore course he was no great shakes. It was his boat and he would call the shots, that was the long and the short of it. 'Not till we've left the harbour,' he murmured, without looking up. Then, as though he'd become aware of our inactivity, he suggested we check the fenders.

'Aye aye captain.'

'Oh, and the life-jackets are below decks.'

After interminable fidgeting, bantering, trying to be busy in imprecise activity, the relief of the whine arrived. It was the moment the conductor's baton taps the stand. Our engine sputtered into abrupt, semi-submerged flatulence. I leaned over and watched the stern's orifice blubber yellowy smoke, spatter a thin blue slick over the opaque water. Upon its edges glimmered reds and indigos, the dirty imitation of a rainbow. Can anything live in harbour water?

Untried at my feet lay a life jacket. I hoped Victor wouldn't notice. I couldn't stomach its coarse touch, much less the damp fabric smell of it. In any case, I was well able to swim.

Feeling encouraged by the vibrations beneath my soles, I began to play out the damp tether as Andrew, unfeasibly tall on the second trawler, walked us along its flank and then held fast so that our bow wheeled about to face the open sea. By the time he leapt back on board, the hull of the trawler had been replaced by slimy harbour granite. Mites flitted about the pubic wrack where the hem of the tide had fallen, where muscles like blue contusions hissed and held fast until the waters returned.

The engine burbled. With each roll, its gargle reverberated as though we were in a tunnel. It might have been a lesson in acoustics, the way the pitch resonated with the gap between hull and harbour wall. Tommy crouched with a pole angled toward the enormous wall, looking absurdly like a 1798 statue. He kept his eyes fixed dog-like on Victor's grey head. He was all set to fend off, and I knew that the instant he did, we would be truly isolated.

But I was calm about it. I was even eager. Victor looked deliberately at each one of us, as proud as Punch. Then he depressed the throttle, the deck juddered, and the indefatigable inboard began to nudge the harbour and the whole town to aft.

Suddenly, you stop struggling.

Only then, the hand eases its clamp.

Barely, and threateningly, the hand eases its clamp. Breath rushes in in short spasms. It rushes through your nostrils, into your chest and out, in and out. It is vile with the intimacy of sweat. Vile with the stink of wet fabrics. You labour, like an asthmatic, to draw it in. To hold it in.

Tongue can taste blood's metal on your teeth now. Your whole mouth is a bruise. Your lips are numbed under the merciless pressure of the hand.

A minute passes. Two.

Next, on your ribcage, the pressure of knees eases, imperceptibly. Threateningly. 'Easy does it. Nobody's going to hurt you.'

You look away. Christ!

You have to find …

'Easy now!'

Somewhere, you can hear the car engine idling, idling above the intolerable noise of their breathing. Only your eyes are free.

Only your eyes are free to move. So you look towards the noise. You look towards it, and you keep every screed of consciousness focused on the clouds of vapour dyed to red in the taillights, where the exhaust is idling, idling.

The indefatigable inboard edged the harbour backwards until we passed squarely between the piers and the whole boat took on the roll of the ocean. The wind was suddenly lively. It had a chilly edge. I hunkered, my fingers on the guy, and watched the markers recede, green, red, asymmetrical. I watched the harbour's mandibles gradually closing. Nearby, to port, a rock dominated by cormorants drifted behind us. Black crucifixions, someone had called them. Who? I was still standing to stern by the tiller, still cradling the water-heavy tie that Andrew had thrown to me. Feeling the world roll beneath me, my body had hunkered and tensed, but I didn't want to sit. I was damned if I was going to be a passenger or anything like it.

Now that we were outside the harbour, the sea was a lively Muscadet which distance turned to jade and then to slate. Earlier I'd felt the sun's heat on my body, but the men had been farting about in the harbour for so long that a scattering of clouds had had time to gather. Their shadows moved like dark herds over the surface. Each time we passed through one I shivered.

Far out, though it was hard to judge distance, there was a regatta, but at this stage of the season Victor had only talked of going out for a practice run. We better make sure the old girl holds together, he'd said. To take my mind off the cold, I tried to make out the letters on the dancing sails. They were the folded wings of cabbage-whites, tiny in the huge expanse of the bay.

'What about your jacket, love? You want to put it on you.'

I looked at Tommy, who'd been seated with the tiller extension between his knees, and who was now rising.

'Here, do you want me to hold it for you?'

'No!' I cried. He'd taken a tiny, clumsy step towards me and had teetered forwards. My forearm held him off. 'No!'

He looked at me, startled. My other hand groped for the lifejacket. 'I'll be fine!'

'Suit yourself,' he shrugged. He backed off, resuming the tiller. Every muscle was tense, and I had to struggle to maintain my balance. My hand had found the lifejacket, but I didn't want it. I didn't want the male stink of its fabric anywhere near me. As Tommy turned his head from me, I stared daggers at a balding tonsure that the wind was mercilessly exposing.

Of course I was being unreasonable. A real bitch. After all he seemed a harmless character. Awkward, a little slower than the other two. A face, as Gill would say, that only a mother could love. But damn it, where was it written I had to love everybody? Where was that part of the deal?

We motored on.

'Right gentlemen,' called Victor over his shoulder. He hastily abutted 'and lady! Are we ready to do some sailing?' At once the engine revs juddered and died.

The silence was overpowering. Not silence. Absence of the mechanical, that was it. The humdrum. Now, instead, the air was full with the bluster of the wind. The wind, slapping its phantom laundry in my face, who'd said that? Where's your memory gone girl? It's the wind section tuning up, I determined, the tinker of shrouds and shackles, the tireless slap of the swell against the hull. Suddenly, the boat had become a live thing, bobbing, pitching, oscillating. Far from silent, it was clamorous, and giddy as a colt.

'Tommy, you look after the tiller. Keep her steady, and the nose close to the wind. Ellen, will you, ahm, will you give Andrew a hand to mount the jib. When you have it tied and ready, signal me. I'll hoist the mainsail.' He was loving this, was Captain Birdseye. The cock of the roost. He'd even grown a neatly trimmed beard since the autumn!

As he spoke he turned to face me, and I could sense his bird's eye taking in the absence of lifejacket. I'd already taken a couple of steps forwards, hoping against hope to slip by unnoticed.

'You haven't put on your jacket.'

'No I...' I knew it was useless. I could feel already the loathsome canvas straps, the dank pouches. 'Fact is,' I tried to laugh, 'I'm a hell of a swimmer.'

'Sorry. It's rules.'

'Suppose you were to knock your head...?' Andrew's interjection from behind me took me by surprise. Feeling it was a miniature betrayal I thanked him with a frosty look. But I was already retreating. I stared hard at Tommy's thinning hair as I bent for the cursed yoke, daring him to turn and say with his eyes I told you so. But he was too busy examining the quick of his well-bitten thumbnail. Probably he was embarrassed.

Andrew was about to do his gentleman's bit when I cut him off. 'I'll be fine!'

But of course I wasn't. Oh no.

It was one of those buoyancy aids with a dangling harness that straps under the crotch, and whether it was tangled or set too tight, my chagrin made me hobble myself on it. I stumbled, teetered, and had to grab onto his arm to prevent myself pitching into the sea.

'Whoop-la!' he said, deftly swinging me upright. He was steady as a mast. He was also being too obviously gallant about the indignity. Fuck you!

Fuck the lot of you! I was so furious I was on the point of tears. I'd managed to skin my leg against the guy, and the smart of it rushed me. Don't let him see! Don't let them…

Tartly, I flung the contraption from me.

'Why don't you sit down?'

'I was *going* to sit down! Jesus!'

I sat.

Discomfiture, like a mutineer, took over the restless boat. I sat, sulking. I hated myself for it. I hated the stupid boat. I hated the stupid lifejacket. I hated the pain that was rushing in waves from my shin and the little white flaps that were fluttering along the edges of the scrape.

The men of course began to be busy about their respective tasks. I was the stupid female. I was the cow who could be counted on to throw a strop. I fixed my eyes on the distant harbour, thankful at least that I'd held in the hot tears. He hadn't seen me weep my indignation. Neither had the others. None of them, ever.

No one, no one had seen me cry. Not even Gill. *Have a good cry girl.* I don't want to cry. *Really, it'll do you good.* I don't. Want. To cry.

I sat still, emotions as unruly as the boat. Their *Nightingale.* I had to sit on my hands. A huge part of me wanted to jump overboard and swim for it.

That I could make the shore I didn't doubt. For several months now, every evening, I'd swum length after length of the municipal pool. It calmed my trembling.

I looked again at the harbour, to gauge the distance. The problem was, their damned boat would overtake me. Then the men's arms would drag me back on board, an ignominious cub dragged from danger. So I sat on my hands, and I brooded.

The boat slapped, skipped, shunted. Two of the men were absorbed in rigging up their toy. Tommy, his back to me, was cradling the tiller arm. How much of a head start would I need?

I stared at a ludicrous strand of Tommy's hair erect and alert as an antenna. Then I was on my feet. The deck seesawed. I crouched, my fingers trailing the boom, my eyes not leaving the hateful back. Would he turn around? Swell after swell of ultramarine hissed up at me. I glanced at the other two, unwatched. Slip in, girl.

And...*what?*

I was sitting, again. But it wasn't cowardice that had held me back. It was the opposite.

After a while, I reached for the jacket with my foot and dragged it towards me. I knew without looking that the men's eyes would be studiously avoiding me, as if we were strangers on a crowded DART. It was laughable. We were bobbing about, a good half-mile from shore, and now the three men were afraid to talk to me, Ellen Greene. Jesus, this fucking boat!

The jacket wasn't as bad as I'd been expecting. It was coarse and cold and vaguely uncomfortable, but at least it didn't smell, or if it did, it was the slightly rubbery smell you get inside a tent. It took me a good couple of minutes to figure the straps and loops, but then, no one was watching. No one was trying to be helpful. Right, girl. You can beat this.

Andrew was crouched to the front of the boat, having pulled the jib single-handed from the hold, and from his expression it was ready to be hoisted. Captain Birdseye was busy doing I know not what exactly with the halyard at the mast, and Tommy, well. Tommy was still inordinately interested in his fingernails. So it was to Tommy I spoke.

'You don't know, is there a first aid box?'

He turned and squinted at me.

'Only I seem to have scraped my leg. When I was doing my ballet stunt there.'

'Show! Is it bad?'

'No, you're grand. Forget it.'

'Here, take the tiller love. I think I seen a box down below.'

'You're grand.'

'It won't take a minute.' He'd already passed the tiller extension to me and before I could speak he'd swung down the steps and disappeared below decks, as agile as an ape.

Managing the tiller gave me a whole new set of problems. Without any forward momentum, we were pretty much at the whim of every bottle-green wave that hefted us over its back. The bow was pointing now at the dissipating regatta, now at the harbour, now at the headland about which ugly clouds were gathering. The sky was by this time entirely overcast. My body was all goose-bumps and sudden shivers, but I paid it no heed. For the moment I just wanted Tommy to return, to take back the demented tiller before either Victor or Andrew noticed the randomness of our orientation.

Then, unexpectedly, Victor began to hoist the mainsail, the boat eased into motion, the tiller pushed against me and with a sibilant rush, steerage became possible. 'What bearing?' I cried, elated.

'What?' Captain Birdseye was non-plussed to see the obstreperous female, and not his Tommy, at the helm. 'Ahm...' He began to look about, a hand shading his eyes. Trying to let on he knew what he was about. 'Why don't you hold a course for that buoy?' I saw what looked a black bag of refuse bobbling in the distance. All the miniature cabbage-whites were streaming past it for shore, electric white against the darkening sky. Beyond them the sea was beaten lead from which a sullen light glimmered.

'If you say so!' I cried. The rush of air and insolent dashes of brine were thrilling and for the moment I was alone.

'Sorry love there's only a bottle of iodine and a bit of cotton wool. There's no plasters or anything.' Tommy's head with its wilful antennae of hair had re-appeared at the top of the stairs. 'Will I get it for you?'

'Sure.' He was gone again almost before I'd spoken.

Hush, hush, hush, called the sea.

'What do you think, shall we give her a little jib?'

The captain's question was directed forwards, at Andrew. Naturally. No point in asking the moody bitch. I didn't catch what Andrew replied, but I saw him scramble quickly to windward. With the mainsail fully up we were already heeling. As he stretched his body out over the waves he smiled back towards me, relieved, I think, to see me involved. Victor glanced doubtfully at me. 'Where did Tommy go?' he called, a hand cupping his mouth. I pointed down the hatch, and then looked past him to the buoy as though our lives depended on my holding that precise course. But I saw him sneak a glance to Andrew, whose length was extending far beyond the gunnel to counter the list. Victor then set his leg squarely against the mast to hoist the jib. It rose in fits and starts, and the whole bow was at once flapping thunderously. The wild sail flailed and boomed in the wind, and a length of untethered rope recoiled in the air like a whiplash.

Tommy's head and shoulders jack-in-the-boxed in front of me. 'They had've secured the sheet!' he cried, and then, in a remarkably quiet tone given the racket of the wayward sail, he added over his shoulder, 'You want to turn her downwind love.'

I did so. He was already hauling the boom in square, and we instantaneously lost power. The jib now fluttered, flapped, furled, but with none of its previous venom. With the boat righted, Andrew was free to scamper forwards to retrieve the rope from the water. He passed it back to Tommy, who did whatever it was had to be done, and then he nodded to me to set her back on course. I caught Victor looking at me, but he glanced away immediately I met his eye.

'They had have secured the sheet before ever they hoisted the jib.'

Tommy's words were low, scarcely a thought. I assumed he was talking to me, but I found when I glanced in his direction he was addressing his hand. 'That augurs well,' I muttered. I have an idea he heard me. If he did, he probably imagined I was mocking the jib fiasco. I hope so.

I pushed the tiller arm out, and the boat swung into a vigorous reach. Soon she had taken up her previous canter, mounting each crest obliquely, rolling in each trough. Then, God knows why, the iodine and cotton-wool must have returned to Tommy's wandering thoughts because he sprang up, glanced at me, nodded at my leg, and once more scuttled down below. I'd forgotten entirely about the scrape, though now of course it smarted. But any pain was swamped by the spasms of cold racking my body, and the euphoria of wild motion. Andrew was now sitting up, and he shouted over to Victor something relating to the weather. So many of his words were carried away that he had to gesture over his shoulder towards the headland, partly obliterated by rippling curtains of grey where a shower had intervened. It all looked rather ominous.

Victor dropped down to the space in front of me. He'd pulled a winch-handle from its sheath with one hand, and with the other hand had coiled the jib-sheet around the lower windlass the wrong way. Without so much as a word to any of us he corrected it, and now began to wind furiously, then to coax it with back and forwards turns. As the jib tightened and groaned, the deck heeled dangerously, throwing more wind-splash into our faces. Pure power surged through the tiller. I thrilled at it. 'Do I hold course for that buoy?' I shouted.

Victor looked hard at me. He nodded, leaned in, called out 'When she passes it you'll need to get her ready to come about. We're going to have to take her back to base.' But he was entirely unable to keep the dubious nuance from his eye. She. The boat. I'd be just as unmanageable.

I wondered was Victor thinking of staying beside me the whole time, at arm's length from the tiller. But with the wind up we were so far heeled over that pots and pans clattered about below decks, and every third wave sluiced liberally over the gunnel. Twice his hand all but touched the tiller to ease it, but he was afraid the bitch might bite. Instead, he shimmied over beside Andrew to throw his weight against the list.

Minutes later, as the black buoy loomed, there were icy needles on the wind. To make matters worse, I knew the minute we rounded the buoy we'd be heading pretty much square into the squall. Why hadn't I taken the waterproofs? If anyone had been near, they would have seen how uncontrollably my body was trembling. We'd heeled once so drastically that, amidst a calamity of falling plates, Tommy had scrambled up, but his back was to me. He was crouching now on the thwart and holding both ends of the jib-sheet as if it was a huge rein and the boat a wild beast we were riding. Unnoticed, Victor was learning from him.

From the helm, unwatched, I watched the three of them, feeling the power that surged through my hand. All were watching the buoy now, as we bore rapidly down on it. All were bracing themselves for the manoeuvre. Planning out their moves. Something welled up in me as I watched them, a raw emotion. It was the last thing on earth I was expecting to feel.

The wind was howling in the shrouds like a banshee and every stay was finely tuned and resonant. *Nightingale* was singing!

'Ready about!' I cried.

'Lee ho!'

With a sudden push, the yacht threw herself to the left and my body to the right. The prone men scrambled over the deck, and the windlasses whined and whirred to the frenzy of frantic ropes. We were faces to the rain.

I felt the gorgeous panic of being, of pure being. I felt exuberant. I looked at the three men hunkered against the rain and I yelled silently into the mounting squall you did it girl by Christ you fucking did it!